3/22

Forever Knight

A Thornton Brothers Time Travel Romance Novel

Book 2

Cynthia Luhrs

This book is a work of fiction. Names, characters, places, and incidents either are products of the author's imagination or are used fictitiously.

Forever Knight, A Thornton Brothers Time Travel Romance Novel

Copyright © 2016 by Cynthia Luhrs

All rights reserved, including the right to reproduce this book or portions thereof in any form whatsoever.

Acknowledgments

Thanks to my fabulous editor, Arran at Editing720
and Kendra at Typos Be Gone.

Chapter One

Kentucky—Present Day

The dingy police station had seen better days. The middle-aged officer barked at Elizabeth, motioning her forward, deeper into the sterile, gray room.

"Name?"

"Elizabeth." Seven. The number of times, counting this one, she'd been arrested. By now she'd thought the police would have sent her through some kind of express line. Or given her some kind of rewards card. Five arrests and the offender gets a t-shirt. She clapped a hand over her mouth to keep from snickering. The bored-looking man would most definitely not be amused.

The officer held up her driver's license and peered

over his glasses.

"Don't be difficult." He let out a long-suffering sigh and pointed to the others waiting their turn. "Full name. And speak up; it's loud in here."

She flinched. *Just tell him and get it over with. They could have named you Sunshine Star.* Elizabeth stood up straight, chin lifted. Her dearest friend wasn't embarrassed about *her* name, so she wouldn't be either.

"Rainbow Elizabeth Smith."

The cop blinked. A grin tugged at his mouth. "Thought I had to be reading this wrong." He peered at the license again. "Talk about a mouthful. Parents some kind of new-age hippies?"

"Something like that."

"I'd be embarrassed too." He took in her clothes. From her sneakers with daisies on them all the way up to her hair. His eyebrows moved independently, like caterpillars crawling across his forehead. Laughter threatened and she bit down on her lip to keep it from escaping.

The cop squinted. "The hair doesn't help."

Elizabeth's shoulders slumped. "The result of way too much wine one night." She looked behind her at Sunshine, patiently waiting her turn. "Never decide it's a good idea to change your hair after a bad breakup, especially if there's wine involved. It doesn't end well."

"You look like a demented fairy princess."

She sighed, not bothering to reply as the next officer

beckoned to her. Her hair would grow out eventually. At least she was rid of Dennis the sponge.

"Did you send the text when they arrested us?" Sunshine sat down beside her, gulping water from a paper cup.

"Yep. I had all the numbers set up so the text should have gone to my lawyer, parents, and Oliver. You?"

Her friend leaned back against the cinderblock wall. "I did, and since it was a prepaid phone, the cops won't get any information."

Gratitude flowed through her as Elizabeth drank the lukewarm water. The last time she'd been arrested, no one gave them water at all. "Our lawyer should be here soon."

Sunshine grinned. "Maybe we'll be out in time to order a pizza for dinner. Busy day at the office tomorrow."

They both worked for a small nonprofit whose primary purpose was to ensure people had access to clean drinking water. She ran through her mental list. Was her camper okay? The vintage home was her baby. Wandering around an auction, she'd fallen in love at first sight. Got it for a steal. Then she'd had it refurbished and dragged it all over the place. From protest to protest. That was how she found herself currently locked up in a tiny town in Kentucky, waiting to be bailed out.

The coal company was going to blast on a pristine

mountain, ruining the drinking water of families who relied on the cool water flowing down from the mountain to their wells. The door to the holding cell opened and an obviously drunk old woman staggered inside.

"Who are all these folk?" The woman cast a cranky look over them. "They're hogging up all the room."

The officer didn't even turn around as he left. "Protestors. Now be quiet, Miss Eloise, and I'll scrounge up some dinner for you."

The woman shuffled over to the cot Sunshine was sitting on and pointed. Elizabeth's friend quickly stood. "Please, sit."

Sunshine sat down cross-legged next to Elizabeth. "Smells like she bathed in whisky."

"My hearing's fine, little lady." The woman peered down at them then leaned forward and touched Elizabeth's hair. "Good gracious, child. Your hands match your hair. The paint goes on the canvas, not in your hair." She laughed and laughed, slapping her knee, until she was crying.

It wasn't that funny. "I was up all night painting signs. Guess I missed a few spots on my hands." There was paint under several nails and a vivid blue streak across Elizabeth's wrist. On her left hand, several colors looked like a rainbow-spotted cheetah had brushed against her.

The woman belched. "Doesn't explain the hair."

Elizabeth self-consciously touched the ponytail. “It’s a long story.”

The woman hummed to herself. After a while she opened one light blue eye. “What’s two girlies like you doing locked up here?”

Sunshine stood and stretched. “We grew up together in California. Went to college and got jobs working for the same company. We protest companies polluting drinking water.” She paced back and forth in the cell, gesturing wildly. “I’ve been arrested ten times and Elizabeth seven.”

Sunshine looked at the woman, a speculative look on her face. Uh oh. Elizabeth knew what was coming.

“We can help you. Have you been unjustly imprisoned?”

The woman cackled, her eyes seeming to disappear into the wrinkles on her face. She slapped her knee. “Naw. Every now and again I go on a walk to talk to my ancestors. There’s times I drink a bit much and end up in town. One of the nice officers brings me here.” The woman sneezed. “I eat a hot meal and in the morning they let me go.”

She touched Elizabeth’s ponytail. “That’s my mountain the damn coal company wants to rape and pillage. So I’m obliged to you both for trying to help.” She reached in the pocket of her dress and came out with a small tin. The dress was a faded calico print, the flowers almost pastel from repeated washings over the years.

"Rock candy?" She held out the tin.

Sunshine took a piece, popping it in her mouth. "Yum. I taste lemon. And mint."

The woman opened her mouth, showing off surprisingly white teeth, given her age. She sucked on a piece of the candy. "My secret recipe. My gran taught me to make it."

"It's delicious." Elizabeth ran her tongue over the bumpy candy.

"I've lived in the holler up on the mountain all my life. Born and raised like my mother and hers before." With the speed of a much younger person, she snatched Elizabeth's hand.

"Got the gift of sight." She ran a gnarled finger across Elizabeth's palm, tracing the lines. "What happened here?"

Elizabeth's wrists were bruised and raw. "From the zip ties when they arrested us. It'll go away in time."

The woman made a noise in the back of her throat, letting Elizabeth know what the woman thought of their treatment. Funny how a noise could convey an entire conversation.

"Now hush. Let the lines speak to me."

Over and over, the woman ran her fingers across Elizabeth's palms. Tracing the lines, muttering to herself. It had been a long day and Elizabeth was tired. Unable to keep her eyes open, she closed them for a moment.

When she woke, Elizabeth and the woman were the only ones left in the cell. The woman stared off into the distance, turning her head when Elizabeth coughed.

“I never seen a hand like yours afore. You will make a long journey.”

She resisted the urge to roll her eyes. What was next—meet a tall, handsome stranger?

“This world is ever-changing. Your destiny is elsewhere. Not in this place.” The woman took Elizabeth’s hands in hers, the skin soft as suede. The subtle scent of herbs filled her nose.

“But know this, child. Where you go, there is no return. Words lie. Look to the actions behind the words and you will find your way.”

Then she dropped Elizabeth’s hands, her chin rested on her chest, and she closed her eyes.

“Wait. Is that it? No handsome stranger?” But the woman was fast asleep and didn’t wake. Well, Elizabeth would have an interesting story to tell when she got home. Her stomach grumbled. If she ever got out of jail.

Chapter Two

England—November 1333

Robert Thornton, Lord of Highworth Castle, cracked a bleary eye and groaned.

"Shut the bloody bed curtains. Are you trying to blind me, old man?"

Featherton huffed, handing him a cup. "You've wasted the day, my lord. 'Tis time to wake."

Feminine giggling filled the chamber. A bare foot stuck out of the covers. Two wenches sprawled across him, barring him from moving. Robert frowned as he drained the cup.

"Go on, then. You know the rules. No staying the night." He almost fell from the bed as he fumbled for the pouch he'd carelessly tossed to the floor yestereve.

His steward grumbled as he picked up the rumpled clothing. A female foot caressed his backside. Sniffing, he made a face that said, *Must I put up with such harlotry?* Featherton could say much with a single glance.

"When shall we see you again, my lord?" The blond one, with hair like the sun, favored Robert with a wink. Only she had difficulty and blinked both eyes, making her look rather like a cross-eyed owl.

The redhead tucked the coins away in her ample cleavage, a saucy grin on her face. "You know where to find us when you wants us again."

Indeed he did, though he would give all the gold in his coffers to wake up in his own chamber with a wife of his own.

The women tittered and whispered as they dressed, casting speculative looks at Robert's steward. The man hurried the wenches out the door, jumping when the redhead pinched his arse on her way out.

Robert couldn't help it—he burst out laughing. Featherton cast a cutting glance his way, one that promised a meager meal, if any. Robert only had two rules. Only the two, yet he'd broken one last night. Seems he'd been too far in his cups yestereve to care.

The first rule: women never stayed the night. The second: no wenches in his bedchamber. Ever.

The last time his youngest brother, Christian, visited nigh on a year ago, he'd asked Robert about the rules.

Mercilessly tormented him.

"Why don't you want them to see your chamber? Do you keep a dead body under the bed? Or perform dark magic?"

Robert didn't appreciate the jest. In truth, he didn't know why. No, that was a lie. The lord's chamber was for the lord and his lady, not wenches he dallied with. The thought of a woman, not his wife in his bed, made his stomach cramp. He was a dolt.

There wasn't a single eligible maiden in all the realm he hadn't called on. By the saints, he'd tried, but there was something wrong with every lass. Some were too tall, others too short, some were too thin, and others too plump. A few slurped their soup and had terrible manners, while others had the makings of ear-splitting shrews. Plenty came with large dowries, and yet it wasn't enough to entice him. Gold he had more than enough of. Mayhap he was destined to live out the rest of his years alone.

Henry and John had found wives, perfectly happy being ordered about. His youngest and eldest brothers hadn't yet taken wives. Christian wanted a large family. Vowed to take a wife once Robert and Edward married. 'Twas only right as youngest he should be last. Edward... Robert expected his stuffy brother to show up with a wife on his arm any day. The man had wept like a woman when he held Anna's wee babe. He'd been talking of heirs and legacy ever since.

Robert padded down the hallway to his chamber, Featherton waiting.

"You stink." The man sniffed. "I've had a bath prepared."

"Delightful." Robert tugged the beautifully embroidered tunic over his head and stalked to the tub, letting the steaming water soothe his aching head. A cup was thrust into his hand. He didn't even open an eye as he sipped the spiced wine.

His steward shaved him and helped him dress for the day, or what was left of it. Edward teased him, saying Robert's clothing, while perfectly acceptable at court, was foolish to wear around Highworth, where there was no one to see it. But Robert disagreed. One should always be well dressed and prepared for new adventures.

The chamber was large and richly appointed. Any woman would find it pleasing, though perhaps a bit masculine for her tastes. But wasn't that what women liked to do? Spend gold and change a home until it pleased them?

Mayhap the problem was he needed a girl from the future. Like Henry and John had found. Halfway through the great hall, he paused. Not only had his brothers found future brides, so had William Brandon and James Rivers. Robert could not fathom what this future girl might look like only that he needed one. And since there were none to be had, he would remain alone.

Hunting, wagering, and wenching. His three favorite things in all the world.

"You look as though you found a bag of gold in the stables, or perhaps a wench with hair of gold." His captain smirked as he saw to his horse.

"I was thinking 'twas time to marry." Robert was gratified to see the man's mouth drop open. Thomas had been with him since they were boys. Fighting together, winning in tourneys, and becoming men in the same bawdy house. Thomas hailed from a minor house and was content to serve as his captain, mostly as he enjoyed wielding his sword.

Robert clapped Thomas on the shoulder. "I will marry when I find a future girl."

"Lower your voice, my lord." Thomas knew *when* his brothers and cousins wives hailed from. Robert looked around the stables to see if any had overheard. Nay, everyone was busy with the tasks of the day. "No one heard."

"You should not say such things. 'Tis not wise to tempt the fates."

Robert scoffed. "What do I care? The fates have done nothing but heap trouble on my head."

His captain crossed himself, looking to the heavens. "I will remind you of this day when you find yourself chained to a girl not of your own choosing."

They made their way out to the lists, the muscles in Robert's arm flexing as he lunged. "'Twill always be my choice. Any woman would count herself favored by fortune to have one as handsome and charming as I."

A few of the garrison knights scoffed. One called out, "Don't you know by now, the girl always chooses the man, not the other way round."

Robert wielded the sword, lunging forward. "Women, the lot of you. You know nothing of lasses. You believe you pay them and they do as you bid. Why should a wife be any different?"

The men jested. Slurs tossed back and forth. Becoming cruder as Robert worked his way through the garrison. He was rather pleased with himself at this idea. The next time Edward sent one of his damnable letters, beseeching him to take a wife, he would respond. Tell his meddlesome brother he would marry as soon as a future girl appeared in his hall.

Content it would never happen, Robert whistled, happier than he'd been in days. 'Twas a fine afternoon. He would hunt, eat, and drink. Letting the days flow into one another, drinking and laughing, until the sun fell for the night and rose again in the morning. He would not dwell on things he could not change. Nor the faces of the dead that haunted his dreams.

Without a care in the world, he called for the stable boy to saddle the black. He was full of joy—and that was what he would continue telling himself until it rang true.

Chapter Three

Elizabeth blinked as she walked out of the jail and into the early morning. The street was deserted except for a few officers coming and going to their shifts. What was that dreadful smell? With a discreet sniff, she recoiled. It was her—the aroma of the jail had seeped into her skin after she'd been locked up for more than fourteen hours. The sun was coming up, turning the sky the color of sherbet. Sunrise and sunset were her favorite times of the day. The church bell at the end of the square rang out, calling worshippers to the early morning service.

"I'm so glad you brought Lulabell. I was worried she'd be towed."

Darla hugged her. "She's fine, and so is the camper. I explained to the guy who owned the furniture store what happened and he said we could pick it up today."

Lulabell was her vintage Beetle. A mechanic whose daughter she'd befriended at a sit-in offered it to her after his darling daughter decided enough with the protests, time to make real money. She went into finance and drove a huge Mercedes. The man had lovingly restored the car, and Elizabeth had fallen in love with the quirky bug at first sight. It was a deep metallic sapphire blue with huge white daisies painted all over it. Talk about an attention getter. The interior matched. Blue with daisies covering the seats. And it coordinated perfectly with her apple-red vintage camper.

Darla held up the keys. "You feel up to driving?"

"I couldn't sleep at all. It was so noisy, and something about the sensation of being behind bars..." Elizabeth shuddered. "It's the worst feeling ever." She held up her hands. "I know. I say every time, no more arrests. Honestly, I don't know how people in jail survive. Without the sun on my face or the freedom to go where I want, and when I want...I think I'd curl up and die."

She hugged Darla tight. "Thank you again for bailing me out. And coming down here with my lawyer. I'm sure by now he's tired of bailing me out. So you drive and I'll relax."

From the police station it was a twenty-minute drive to the furniture store where the camper was parked. Darla chatted while she drove, catching Elizabeth up on life. Her dear friend was a lawyer in private practice. She had recommended Elizabeth's present lawyer, saying he had more experience. Darla's two older sisters shared the firm, taking on a variety of interesting cases. As they drove, something peeking out from the seat caught Elizabeth's eye. It was a glossy magazine with a knight in shining armor on the front.

"What's this? Is it yours? Boy oh boy, if all medieval knights looked like this, I'd be all about giving up hot showers."

Darla pushed her glasses up. "It was the strangest thing, I found it under the windshield wipers on the car. I meant to throw it away, but with all the commotion, I hadn't gotten around to it. Who leaves a Renaissance faire magazine under somebody's windshield wiper?"

Elizabeth flipped through the pages, stopping to read an article on swords. Ever since she was a child, she'd load up at the library, devouring books. After she'd worked her way through the children's section, she'd read anything she could get her hands on. Turning the page, a jolt shot through her. The advertisement took up the entire page, the picture pulling her in, tempting her to read the accompanying text.

It was the pinnacle of a princess castle straight out of a fairytale. More ornate than she had ever imagined as a child. Someone with a serious royalty complex must have designed the place. And the countryside—it was breathtaking. All the verdant green, gardens, and the surrounding landscape... Her fingers itched to pick up a paintbrush.

She was so busy imagining herself walking through the grounds that she almost missed it. The advertisement was actually a contest. It seemed all she had to do was write an essay, and the winner would spend an entire week in an authentic English castle. Her excitement mounting, Elizabeth read on.

“Listen to this, Darla...the winner of the contest will enjoy a week at Highworth Castle located near Sutton. The castle has been privately owned and beautifully maintained... Can you believe it? Look at this.” Elizabeth waved the magazine in front of Darla’s face.

“Driving here, remember?” Her friend looked over. “I don’t know; it looks like a wedding cake designer threw up and a castle came out. Since when do you want to stay in a drafty old castle?”

“Only since I was a little girl and dreamed of being a princess with my very own castle. And, of course, the castle came equipped with a dragon and a handsome prince. Rooms with no purpose other than my enjoyment.” She sighed. “I know it’s silly. Castles and princes are so out of reach for most people that they might as well be a fairytale. But a girl can dream.”

Chapter Four

The tables were pushed against the walls. Men bedded down for night in the hall as Robert moved amongst them like a spirit, making his way down to the cellars. Which also served as a dungeon as needs be. In the darkest time of night, when he was unable to sleep, he would prowl the rows, counting the casks and jugs until he was tired enough to return to his chamber. The castle was asleep, quiet except for the men on guard.

As he was counting the third row, the sound of wood scraping against stone had him drawing his sword. The door to the tunnels swung open, and the blade stopped a hairsbreadth from the man's neck.

"Not a verra warm welcome, now, is it?" The rich Scottish burr filled the room, echoing off the stone.

Robert re-sheathed his sword, grimacing. "You

almost lost your pretty head. How did you know about the passageway?"

"Ye told me about it one night long ago."

The Scot stumbled and Robert held up a torch. "What is amiss? You come to Highworth in the dead of night not by the door but through the tunnels. 'Tis not safe for you here." He squinted, noting wet spots on the man's plaid.

Connor McTavish took three steps before collapsing on the stone floor. Robert swore as he knelt down. Up close, Connor smelled of war. River water and mud, unwashed skin, and the stench of old and new blood. The man's normally ruddy skin was tinged with gray.

"Bloody hell." Robert did not have time for such trouble. The man's eyes fluttered. He reached up and, with surprising strength, grabbed hold of Robert's tunic.

"Ye owe me a debt. A life. Or have ye forgotten?"

Robert cursed again. "I have not forgotten," he said stiffly. A year ago, he'd been in an establishment of questionable reputation with several friends. The drink and women were plentiful as they wagered through the night, falling deeper and deeper into their cups. He would never forget how the night ended. "Much as it wounds me to admit, I would have died had you not been there." Robert snorted. "Though even the great McTavish himself could not have dispatched eight men on his own."

The Scot grinned. "Perhaps. Perhaps not. Good thing

you were too bloody stubborn to die."

"Mayhap I should fetch a looking glass so you can see one who is truly stubborn."

"The church would not care for such an object. You are vain enough without admiring your form all day and night." The Scot chuckled then sputtered, spitting out blood. Wincing, he let go of Robert's tunic. "I call the debt due." The man went silent.

Robert leaned close, relief spreading through him when he felt breath coming from Connor. "Damn you, McTavish." He stood, looking down at the warrior wanted by many, including his king. The Scot had killed many English soldiers. To harbor him was treason. Robert's brothers and wives would be in danger as would all of those under his protection at Highworth. Robert had not forgotten all those years ago, what John had cost the family. They'd lost all. Lands, titles, gold.

If he kept Connor McTavish hidden, the Thorntons would lose their lives if anyone found out. No one would be safe. But a debt was a debt. And his damnable knightly honor demanded he pay no matter the risk. Stomping about made him feel a bit better. With a deep breath, he softly knocked on the door.

Featherton stood there fully dressed. "My lord."

"Do you sleep in your clothes?"

The man scowled. "How may I serve his lordship this fine eve?"

Robert chose to ignore the sarcasm. "'Tis important.

Connor is in the wine cellar."

Not even a raised brow. Featherton stepped out of the room, closing the door and striding down the corridor. He woke a small girl sleeping in the kitchens.

"Janet, wake up, girl."

The child sat up, rubbing her eyes.

"Go and fetch Thomas. Bring him alone to the cellar. No one else, understand?"

She nodded and scampered off. Robert watched her go. "Still not speaking?"

Featherton looked at the empty doorway. "No, my lord. The healer said the child had seen such horror she may never speak." He shook his head. "We do not know all that happened to her."

Robert remembered finding the child hiding in a bush. He was after a stag and there she was, curled up like a fox kit, drenched in blood. The child blinked up at him and held out her arms. Never uttered a word. At the castle, she wouldn't go with anyone else until he reassured her all would be well. Many times he found her trailing after him, but still she did not speak.

Thomas met them in the cellars. "You cannot help him. 'Tis treason." His captain of the guard looked down at the Scot and cursed.

Robert knew the feeling well. "I owe him a debt, Thomas."

"Give him gold and send him on his way." Thomas prodded the big Scot with a booted foot. "Perhaps he will die. It would be for the best."

Featherton sniffed. "There is a large price on his head. Many would turn him in for the gold."

"Nay. He stays." Robert took the man's arms. "We will put him in the empty chamber next to mine. Tell no one." He looked to his steward. "Janet can tend to him. We keep him locked away until he is healed enough to leave."

"Why, Robert?" Thomas looked at him. "You risk all for a Scot who would slit our throats in our beds."

"Not now."

Janet tugged on Robert's tunic.

"Everyone is still asleep?"

She nodded.

"Thank you, lass."

Robert bent down. "Help me move him." They carried Connor silently through the hall and up to the chamber. Robert suppressed a chuckle at the number of weapons Featherton piled on the trunk at the foot of the bed. Two swords, two daggers, and four dirks.

"No wonder he was so heavy," the steward said as he laid the last dirk on the pile of weaponry.

Janet silently entered the room and set about cleaning the man's wounds. She motioned them over, pointing to the slashes on his chest and the hole in his shoulder and arm. Robert threw the ruined silk under tunic into the fire. Arrows couldn't pierce silk. The point went in, taking the silk with it. He could see a bit of the fabric in the man's shoulder. 'Twas good—it could be removed without leaving any of the arrow behind.

"Damn it to hell." Thomas ran a hand through his hair. "He needs a healer."

Robert looked to Featherton. "Wake the witch."

Thomas crossed himself. "Nay. He may be a bloody Scot, but we cannot. She will steal his soul."

"You are an old woman. The healer will keep our secret, though she may turn you into a frog for crossing yourself in her presence." Seeing the expression on his captain's face, Robert laughed. "I should not jest. In truth, I do not know if she is healer or witch, and I care not."

Robert looked out the window into the blackness. In a few hours it would be morning. "Connor McTavish saved my life." He turned to face the men. "'Twas a year ago during winter. Eight men caught me unaware in the inn. I was...unsteady. The Scot saved me. Fetched a healer. Stayed with me until the fever passed and I healed." He blew out a breath. "After, when I was still weak as a babe, he tracked down the three men who had escaped. Killed them one by one." He stared down at the man. "If he had not raised his blade, I would be dead."

Thomas cursed. "You told everyone you spent the winter with a woman."

Robert shrugged. "Even then Connor had a price on his head. And my pride was injured."

"I will fetch the healer," Featherton said as he left the

room.

"Not a word to anyone." Robert looked from Thomas to Janet. Both nodded. "Janet, you will aid the healer."

The girl nodded and went back to cleaning Connor's wounds. Janet cleaned and helped in the kitchen. She tended minor wounds, had a soft touch. The child would grow up to be a healer; Robert knew it deep in his bones. He should think on asking the healer to take up residence at Highworth. Teach Janet.

Until Connor was gone, it was dangerous for all. Not just at Highworth, but for his brothers and their families. His cousins as well. Everyone must stay away. 'Twas the only way to keep them safe.

Chapter Five

"Mom? Where are you guys?" Elizabeth listened to the static on the phone as her mom's voice faded in and out before finally becoming clear.

"Rainbow, darling. Your father and I are in Peru, but not for long. We're planning our next adventure. We're off to India. Seeking enlightenment. An entire year of traveling around the country and spending time with gurus. Doesn't that sound fantastic?"

Elizabeth loved her parents but they were the flightiest people on the planet. "It sounds great, Mom. I was wondering if you guys might be coming home after India?"

She explained what had happened, the latest arrest. How she felt she wasn't making enough of a difference anymore.

Her dad's rich baritone voice came on the line, filling her with warmth. "Sweetheart, your mother and I think you just need a change to shake things up a bit. Sorry, honey, we're not coming home. Didn't we tell you? We're planning to travel the world. Who knows if we'll ever be back."

There was a muffled conversation and then he was back. "You're welcome to come out and join us..."

Elizabeth knew they loved her, but truly didn't want her to join them. They were the happiest when they were together, just the two of them. That was why they'd raised her to be independent, they told her, so she could carve her own life out of this world. As her mom liked to say, every baby bird must leave the nest and fly away. Only in this case, her parents were the ones flying away.

"I appreciate it, Dad. I was thinking of taking a trip to England, a little time off. Maybe when I'm there, I might come see you both for a few days." No matter if she won the contest or not, Highworth Castle had gotten under her skin.

"Wait a minute, honey. Your mom has something she wants to tell you."

"Your father says you're thinking of going to England? What a marvelous idea." Her mother's laugh tinkled through the phone, bringing her close. From all the noise, it sounded like her parents were walking through some kind of marketplace.

"If you do go to England, make sure you visit

Huntington Castle. It's our old family castle. We had some moldy old ancestor, what was his name? Oh yes, Captain Rawlins Huntington. He lived, let me think...I believe it was around the mid-1600s. Its all ruins, been that way for hundreds of years. Nothing much to see but if you're there anyway, pop over."

"How come you never told me about him? I didn't know we had a family castle." Excitement flooded through Elizabeth. First the old woman in the cell, then the magazine, and now this revelation from the parental units. It was a clear sign from the universe.

"You know, you look like your ancestor, Merry Huntington. Apparently all of the Huntington women share the curly hair and green eyes. The men ended up with blond hair and brown eyes. Anyway, she was a direct descendant of Rawlins, but from what I understand he never married. Too many greats to keep track of. Merry was considered quite scandalous. Supposedly we inherited our penchant for adventure from her."

"I don't remember ever seeing a portrait of either of them."

A sigh sounded over the line like the wind in the trees. "We had them. Remember the fire? You were only five, but the whole house burnt up. The portraits were in the attic. We lost everything. You know, the fire was a blessing. Losing everything forces you to reconsider your life. Before it happened, your father and I were terribly materialistic. Afterwards we realized how lucky we were not to have died, and that's when we decided to simplify our lives. A year later we started traveling about."

"Grandma never said anything about our family tree."

"Oh, you know your grandmother. She didn't want to encourage your wildness…" Her mother trailed off.

Elizabeth wondered if her mother felt bad, leaving her with her grandmother for so long while they traipsed around the world. Though really, she hadn't minded. Whenever they came back, they had some interesting item they'd found and tons of stories. Both of her parents were more like a fun aunt and uncle than real parents. The other kids at school had parents who attended their games, brought cupcakes to school, and were always around.

"My mother convinced us not to take you out of school and drag you all over the world. I told her we would home-school you, but you know your grandmother—she believed in a rigid schedule and a formal education."

Horns and yelling sounded across the line. Her mother's voice turned soft. "We did what we thought was right. No sense dwelling in the past. But one thing I know for sure: the sense of adventure is as strong in you as it is in your father and I. Your grandmother? Somehow the adventure bug and curly hair skipped her.

A homebody through and through. I should go; there's some sort of accident up ahead. Lots of yelling."

"Wait, Mom. What happened to Merry?"

The laugh on the other end traveled the line, wrapping her in a hug, and Elizabeth's throat closed up. "I almost forgot. And I really shouldn't be laughing; it isn't funny. She was hanged at Execution Dock in Wapping for piracy in May of 1701. The story goes she put the rope over her neck herself. Swung next to the infamous Captain Kidd. She never sailed with him. They were on different ships. You know, she dressed as a man and sailed with a rather bloodthirsty crew for years. Lived an eccentric life, to say the least."

"I wish I could have met her." Elizabeth was stunned. She had no idea her ancestor was so fascinating.

"Rainbow, darling. Embrace change; it's good for the soul. No matter what you decide, have fun and live life to the fullest. Kisses."

And with that, her mother was gone. Elizabeth didn't even have time to say goodbye. It was settled. If she won the contest, she'd have an all-expenses-paid trip to England. And if she didn't, she was going anyway. Her boss had made it clear it was time for her to move on. One or two arrests were fine, but by the time you got to seven, the company started to get uncomfortable, thinking Elizabeth was doing too much, going too far. With seven weeks of vacation time coming, she could take a nice, long trip. Maybe it was time for something new. She'd become so frustrated by companies that weren't held accountable for the wrongs they committed.

When the phone rang, her intuition told her to hurry. She jumped out of the shower, dripping water across the floor of the campground facilities, and fumbled with the locker door, searching for the cell phone. "Hello?"

"Miss Elizabeth Smith?" The voice was oh so very English. "Your essay was brilliant. I'm calling to offer you a full week, all expenses paid, at Highworth Castle."

Elizabeth squealed as the voice on the other end changed her life.

"I can't believe I won."

The voice went on. The man provided her with all the details. She wrote them down, her mind racing a hundred miles a minute.

"We apologize for the short notice, but the owner has a few eccentricities. Are you sure you'll be able to make it?"

"Oh, I'll make it. I'll see you in two weeks."

She jumped up and down, screaming and yelling, and a few of the other campers averted their eyes and hurried to leave the crazy woman alone.

Back at the camper, she rummaged in a drawer. When she came outside and plopped down at a nearby picnic table, a small boy and girl were looking at her, their eyes huge. Guess the singing was a bit much. She smiled at them and opened a journal. Colored pens and stickers ready. It was time to plan.

Thanks to her parents' influence, she always had an up-to-date passport, and with her living situation it wasn't like she had a lease or mortgage to worry about. All she had to do was ask Darla if she could leave Lulabell and the camper with her while she was overseas.

England. A fairytale castle. The old woman had been right. She said Elizabeth was going to take a journey. Wrapped up in a blanket, she sipped a chai tea, running her fingers over the scarred wood of the picnic table. Who did the initials belong to? So many lives coming and going. It was in the fifties today. The sun warmed her and melted the last of the snow on the ground. The brisk air invigorated her as Elizabeth listed everything she wanted to do on her trip.

Darla was one of her oldest friends. Thank goodness she lived in Kentucky. She was at Churchill Downs when she got Elizabeth's text. She was a veterinarian and was looking in on one of the horses. There would be plenty of room on the farm where Darla and her husband lived. Wait until Elizabeth told Sunshine. Of course, she'd have to admit to her friend she'd been right about the old woman they met in jail.

How exactly had the woman worded the pronouncement? Something about her not being able to return? That was silly. England was only a plane ride away. She could easily come back whenever she wished. Guess the woman couldn't get everything right.

Who knew? Maybe she would meet a handsome stranger while she was traveling. Find her own happily ever after. It was going to be a grand adventure. And with that thought, Elizabeth decided she'd fly in a day early and visit the site where her ancestor was hanged. After her week of luxury, she'd visit the old family castle.

It was time to make a few changes. She called her boss, gave her two weeks' notice, and was inordinately pleased with herself. Who knew, maybe she'd stay in England. Create her own adventure like her ancestor. Without the whole hanging part, of course.

Chapter Six

Robert nodded to the man on guard as he strode into the chamber. “How is he?”

The healer and young Janet hovered over Connor. The man mumbled and thrashed in his sleep, lines of pain etched across his face. Robert flinched, seeing the damage inflicted upon the Scot. So many wounds, the stitching dark in the light of the fire.

The healer attended him without looking at Robert. “He has a fever. So he may live or he may not. Only the fates know.” She stood and stretched. “Janet will tend him. I have left her with herbs, told her what to do. I have done all I can. The rest is up to him.”

Robert gave her a few coins. They disappeared into the pouch at her waist. Her hair was silver, as were her eyes, yet her face was unlined.

"I know who he is. Do not fear, my lord." She saw something in his face and patted his arm. "He saved your life, therefore I will keep him secret."

"I thank you. No one can know he is here." He walked her to the door, pausing. "We have no healer at Highworth. Would you consider coming to the castle?"

She thought for a moment. "I have my cottage in the woods, but I fear 'tis no longer safe. For I have seen a great war coming, a war that will last a hundred years." She stared off into the distance for so long that Robert wondered if she was going to say anything else. "Are you not afraid of me?"

"I care not if you are witch or healer." Then he chuckled. "The men think you can turn them into animals."

The woman merely blinked at him. "Yes, I will be your healer."

He inclined his head to her. "I will send men to escort you home. They will wait while you pack and bring you back here." He let out a breath. "With Connor here, 'tis not safe for any of us. If you prefer to wait until he is gone..."

"Nay, Robert Thornton. There will be interesting doings here at Highworth. I would not miss them."

"You are under my protection, such as it may be, Mistress Adeline." Watching her go, Robert thought about her words. There was always a war. What difference did it make if it was a year or a hundred years? He no longer cared. And if things got any more interesting, he'd take to his bed with a cask and not come forth until spring.

Janet tried to force the healer's brew down Connor's throat. He knocked the cup away and mumbled in his sleep. The young girl looked ready to weep.

"I will hold him down whilst you make him drink." Robert caught a whiff of the brew and wrinkled his nose. "Smells foul."

The young girl pointed to Connor's mouth.

"Aye. He'll drink." Robert took hold of the Scot's shoulders, holding him firm while the girl tilted his head up, pouring the brew down his throat. Robert pinched Connor's nose closed, forcing him to swallow.

After dinner, a messenger appeared in the hall with a missive from Robert's brother, Edward.

"Show him to the kitchens and see that he is fed." A servant led the messenger away. Robert would compose a reply and send the man back with it in the morn.

Rabbie trailed along behind him. "What does it say? Are your brothers coming to visit? I should like to see John."

"You have an unhealthy curiosity for a lad." Robert made his way to his solar, the boy on his heels. As he entered, Robert turned. "You might as well come in or you'll plague me the rest of the day, won't you?"

Rabbie's face brightened. "Aye, my lord."

Robert read through the letter. He scratched out a

reply informing Edward he had friends arriving who would remain for a sen'night. Then Robert told him he needs repair his hall and one of the chambers, so he had no time to see to his brothers, nor did he wish them to eat through his meager larder. Would it be enough to keep them away?

He added a line saying he would make the journey once the repairs were done. Avail himself of Edward's hospitality. Visit each brother and enjoy their fine wenches. Once Connor was gone, it would be safe for his family to visit, but not until then.

It was bad enough his friends were arriving. He could not send them back at this late notice; there would be too many questions. Suspicions raised. One of the men arriving, Lord Radford, spent a great deal of time at court and was a terrible gossip. 'Twas all Robert needed. He knew the risk was great, but he saw no other way.

The boy fidgeted, wandering around the room. Robert sealed the letter with his ring and handed it to the boy. "Take this to the messenger."

The boy's face fell and Robert suppressed a chuckle. "Nay, they are not coming to visit until the repairs are complete. We have other guests, remember?"

The boy grimaced, "One of them lords was sniffing around Joan."

Robert arched a brow, waiting.

"Joan works in the laundry. I'm going to marry her in a few years."

Everyone was interested in getting married. Everyone but Robert.

Chapter Seven

The next two weeks passed in a blur as Elizabeth worked overtime to finish up odds and ends and train her replacement at work. Before she knew it, she was packed and driving Lulabell and the camper to Darla's horse farm. Sunshine would be there as well. So her last few days in the States would be spent with her best friends.

Darla's husband already had the horses saddled when Elizabeth woke the next morning. After a big breakfast, the three of them headed out for a morning ride. The smell of hot chocolate filled the wintry air. Elizabeth's horse was chestnut brown with a white spot on his forehead that looked like a heart. The trio was bundled up against the cold, a riot of color against the snowy backdrop.

"I love riding through the snow. Everything's so quiet and clean." Sunshine was wearing a bright orange faux-fur coat with a purple scarf and red gloves. Oh, and her boots were bright yellow. She looked like a rogue cartoon character.

"I hope I get a chance to go riding in England. I can't thank you enough for teaching me how to ride." Elizabeth thought her hair was color enough, and had dressed in all black.

Darla patted the white horse. The animal blended into the landscape, making it look like she was floating on air. "Thank David. I didn't even know I liked horses until I married him." She shifted in the saddle to look at both of them as she grinned. "When are the two of you going to settle down and get married? I can't be the only one. Thought we were the three musketeers."

Sunshine frowned. "But how did you choose? There are so many wonderful men out there waiting for us."

"Your problem is you love all men." Darla brushed a clump of snow off her shoulder as Elizabeth laughed.

"Yeah, Sunshine. All shapes and sizes. Every hair color; it doesn't matter. As long as they make you laugh, you love them."

"Give me more choices." Sunshine grinned. "Think about staying in England for good. Then when I've dated every eligible guy in the U.S., I'll come for a visit and work my way through England."

"And Scotland." Darla giggled. "Talk about fantastic

accents."

Elizabeth turned in the saddle to look at her friends. "Why stop there? After the United Kingdom, how about Australia and New Zealand?"

"All of Europe, while you're at it."

Sunshine stuck her tongue out. "Funny. Very funny, you two."

It was midmorning when Darla slowed her horse. "Let's stop here. There's something I want to show you both."

They tied the horses to a nearby tree. The path was well traveled: various animal tracks crisscrossed back and forth, making it look like an animal rush hour. Darla led them through the trees into a small clearing.

Elizabeth let the sun warm her face. "How perfect. It's like someone ripped a page out of a fairytale and brought the scene to life." The pond was completely iced over except for one end, where a tiny waterfall kept the water flowing. The surrounding branches and shrubbery were encased in ice, turning the entire tableau into a winter wonderland. As the three of them soaked in the beauty of the spot, a family of bunnies hopped by, their brown coats contrasting with the snow. There was a flat rock, clear of snow from the sun. They stretched out, drinking hot chocolate, and Elizabeth knew she'd never forget the magical morning.

The rest of the time passed quickly, and before she knew it, she was behind the wheel of Lulabell, on her way to the airport.

"Are you sure you want me to drive your baby while you're gone?" Sunshine stretched in the passenger seat, huge rhinestone-encrusted sunglasses obscuring half her face.

"I'm sure. It's good for her to be driven at least once a week, and since I don't know how long I'll be gone, I'd really appreciate it."

"You're not booking a return ticket?" Sunshine looked interested. "Are you turning into your parents? Going to start posting pictures from exotic locales? Calling once in a while and making us traipse across the world to visit?"

Elizabeth laughed. "I don't know about all that, just thought I'd take some time. Decompress and figure out what comes next."

Sunshine pushed her sunglasses down her nose to peer at Elizabeth. "Then again, maybe you should put that boundless energy into finding Mr. Right. You've had a rough patch after Dennis. I swear he made an art of forgetting his wallet. It's time you met a guy that sees the goodness in you. One that can take care of you for a change." She brightened and waggled her eyebrows. "Maybe he'll be a lawyer, come to bail you out after a protest, and you'll fall madly in love surrounded by bars and puke-green walls."

"Ha ha, very funny." Elizabeth unloaded the bag and backpack and turned to hug her friend. Sunshine's blond hair blew in the wind, causing several double takes from various men entering the terminal.

"Are you sure there isn't anything else you need? Got everything on your list?"

"For someone named Sunshine, you worry an awful lot. I'll be fine, and if I need anything I can always go shopping. It's not like I'm going somewhere where they don't have stores."

"Or Wi-Fi."

They laughed.

"I'll miss you. Don't forget to let me know when you decide you've had enough of England and you're ready to come back."

"You know I will. I'm thinking maybe a month or so. I'll text you when I know my plans."

Elizabeth made her way into the terminal, excitement rising. Even the horribly long lines to pass through security didn't bother her. A real castle, and it was all hers for an *entire week*. Could things get any better?

The sound of passengers moving about woke Elizabeth. Yawning, she stretched, careful not to hit the man beside her.

"I can't believe it. You slept the entire trip. How do you do it?" He looked annoyed she'd been able to sleep.

"Ever since I was little I've been able to sleep anywhere. Planes, trains, cars. It doesn't matter. I close my eyes and I'm out. Makes flying more bearable."

"I can't even sleep like that when I take a sleeping pill. You here for work?" The man's accent made her want to listen to him all day. He had been in the States for business, working for a large pharmaceutical company. When he complained Americans couldn't make a good cup of tea to save their lives, she'd refrained from complaining about leaving behind her beloved Lucky Charms cereal. You had to adapt to the place, embrace the culture, so goodbye favorite childhood cereal. Maybe she'd become a fan of beans for breakfast.

She told him about her work and how she was taking some time off. "So that's how I won a week at a castle. I'm so excited. I've never stayed in a castle before."

"Where?"

They chatted while collecting their things, waiting for

their turn to disembark. Other passengers grumbled at what was taking so long, impatient to get on with their day.

"Highworth. It's near Sutton."

The man made a face. "I know it. My wife likes the place, but to me it rather looks like someone got a little carried away with the icing."

"I know, right? But I have to admit, it's kind of charming in its overdone way. I can't wait to see the inside."

As they made their way into the terminal, he handed her an umbrella. "Always carry a spare. Enjoy your trip."

"Thank you. Now I don't have to buy one." The terminal was well marked, and she quickly cleared customs then found her way outside, where she met the driver. The sponsors of the contest had offered her the car and driver a day early, which she thought was really nice of them. The guy stood there in a uniform, holding a sign with her name on it.

"I'm Elizabeth Smith."

The man took her bags and opened the door of the dark sedan for her. "Where to, miss?"

"I'd like to go to Wapping and the Museum of London Docklands."

"Straight away."

On the way, she read through the documentation she'd printed out before she left. The driver promised to pick her up before dinner so she could check in at the hotel and get settled. With her trusty black backpack slung over one shoulder, she was ready to explore. The museum had an exhibit called Sailortown, which sounded interesting. It was supposed to be an immersive display re-creating the atmosphere. Back in the day, Sailortown was a narrow strip of taverns, slums, and houses situated on the north bank of the Thames, downriver from the Tower of London. It was the center for the merchants of the time with networks extending around the world. From China to Australia, and to the Caribbean and Hudson Bay. From what she read, the merchants were vital in keeping the Navy supplied for their voyages. Had Merry walked these same streets before she met her end?

Execution Dock was where Merry Huntington took her last breath. Elizabeth felt it was important to see the spot, pay her respects to the ancestor who'd gifted her with curly hair and a spirit of restlessness.

What must it have been like? The rope around her neck, the crowds jeering in the square. Elizabeth shuddered. To acclimate herself to the time change, she planned to stay up until her regular bedtime tonight. Seeing the place where Merry died, Elizabeth couldn't believe she'd gotten away with dressing as a man. More likely, the crew knew but chose to accept her.

The air coming off the water was frigid, and she was glad she'd dressed warmly. Her jeans were tucked into knee-high black boots, the sweater a dark gray wool.

The gloves and scarf were cream colored, which was good, considering her hair added enough color for the whole outfit. Never one to wear a hat, she'd attracted plenty of looks due to the pastel colors. No matter what, she'd never fool around with her hair again after a breakup. As if to protest, a purple curl blew in front of her face and she sighed, tucking the lock behind her ear.

By the time the driver picked her up, she was frozen halfway through. As she slid into the darkened interior of the car, a cup of steaming tea was waiting for her.

"Thank you so much. This is exactly what I needed."

"I figured as much. A spot of tea will warm you up a bit. I'll pick you up at nine tomorrow. It's about an hour drive to Highworth."

An honest-to-goodness castle. She rubbed her hands together, thinking of exploring the rooms, touching objects that belonged to people long gone. Wondering about their day-to-day lives. Maybe something at the castle would help her figure out what came next in her own life.

After she checked in to the hotel, Elizabeth popped into a pub across the street. There was an open table by the fireplace and she inhaled a hearty dinner of beef stew with crusty bread and a pint to wash it all down.

Warm and full, she went back to the hotel, took a nice, hot shower, and fell into bed, eyes fluttering closed before her head hit the pillow. As she fell asleep, her last thoughts were of Highworth.

Chapter Eight

The black sedan turned a corner and Highworth Castle came into view, making Elizabeth squeal.

The driver jumped, the car swerving a bit to the left. She bounced up and down in the seat. “Sorry. I’m just so excited. It really does look like some kind of maniacal wedding cake come to life.”

The guy chuckled but refrained from commenting on his employer’s home. California had been Elizabeth’s home until she left high school. Then her grandmother inherited a house in Kentucky from an old sweetheart. A man she’d dated before she married Elizabeth’s grandfather. The man had never gotten over her grandmother, and when he passed had left her the house and plenty of cash. Elizabeth went to college in Kentucky, found a job after graduation, and worked all the time, convinced the travel bug had skipped her as well.

Living in Kentucky, winter had become her favorite time of year. The cold and the snow turning the landscape into a winter wonderland. There was nothing like a horseback ride through the snow as she watched the sky turn to fire. She'd been so busy with work that her passport had gathered dust in a drawer until she'd won the contest.

The driver parked outside the castle walls. He helped her out of the car. "We walk from here."

As they passed through the gates, she touched the walls, a sense of déjà vu flowing through her. "I'd like walls and a gate like these to keep those door-to-door sales guys away."

He grinned. "And archers on the battlements."

"Exactly."

"The walls are forty feet high and fifteen feet thick. The portcullis is closed every night, so if you're not back by eleven, you'll be stuck outside."

She touched the grooves in the wall, imagining the gate slamming closed, trapping her. "What are they made out of?"

"Oak and iron."

Unfortunately, she could imagine all too well the iron spikes on the bottom landing on the enemy. Picking up the pace, she passed the driver, ignoring the chuckle. Maybe in the spring she could come back to see the gardens in bloom. In the pictures they'd looked breathtaking. Now the landscape was sleeping, waiting to come to life again when the weather turned. The gardens were laid out in a formal design, and she itched to walk through them, positive there would be a secret garden waiting to be discovered.

The huge wooden doors to the castle opened, and an older man wearing a dark suit came out to greet them. He looked to be in his mid-seventies.

"To the rose room?"

"Thank you, Francis."

The driver smiled at her. "I'll take your bags up, miss. Have a lovely stay."

"I will, thank you."

The man in the dark suit with bright blue eyes clasped his hands before him. "Miss Elizabeth Smith. Welcome to Highworth." He sounded very serious when he said, "I am Featherton. My family has served Highworth since 'twas built." His eyes twinkled, "I read your essay. A lovely piece. We're glad to have you for the week."

"I still can't believe I won." To his credit, he pretended not to notice her hair. Sure, she could have gotten it colored back, but she'd run out of time and decided to take care of it one day when she was out and about or when she returned home.

She followed him inside the castle, telling herself to close her mouth and not act like a country mouse come to the city for the first time. It was as ornate and over the top inside as it was outside. There were priceless tapestries on the walls—walls covered with elaborate wainscoting and what looked like silk fabric in a vivid shade of royal blue. From the inside she almost forgot she was in a castle, which was slightly disappointing. A small part of her had hoped for gray stone walls and torches. Perhaps a big, shaggy dog in front of the hearth.

The space was luxurious, the smell of hothouse flowers scenting the air. This wasn't at all what she'd expected. It was like being inside a mansion. The floors were tiled in ornate patterns and covered with sumptuous-looking rugs that she was afraid to step on, for fear she'd soil them with her muddy boots.

"This is the great hall. After you've unpacked, perhaps the lady would like to sit by the fire. Martha will bring tea and biscuits."

"That sounds divine. This place is amazing." There were dining tables lined up in a row with benches and high-backed chairs. Enough to easily seat fifty or more people. At the end of the cavernous room was a raised dais where she could easily picture the lord of the castle sprawled out in a chair, looking down on all that was his. Resisting the urge to shout "off with their heads," she followed Featherton through the ornate room.

"The kitchens are there. Breakfast is served at eight, luncheon at noon, cocktails at five, and dinner at seven." The man sniffed. "The cleaning women were here yesterday, so other than Martha and I, you won't see anyone about."

He opened a set of doors, through which she spied a masculine-looking study. More rugs from faraway lands, dark green walls covered with paintings surrounded by thick gold frames, and the desk. The desk alone made her drool, pulled a thread inside, unraveling a need to put down roots with this desk at its center. She wanted this desk something fierce.

"If you'll follow me, the library is this way."

Reluctantly, she tore her eyes away from the desk, the temptation of a library pulling her forward. Elizabeth thought she might pass out from bliss. The reality was so much more than her imagination. He opened the doors with a flourish and her dreams burst forth in full Technicolor. The room was two stories high, with an ornate iron staircase to the second floor. There were so many books, she could read one a day and never finish them all. Leather-bound volumes, old, new, books strewn about and piled everywhere. Books as far as the eye could see.

"I think I've died and gone to heaven. I may never leave this room the whole time I'm here."

Featherstone huffed. "The room is disorganized. One of the village girls left before she could finish ordering the shelves. You may read any of the books except the ones on the second floor. They are extremely old and should not be handled."

"No problem; there are more than enough books on the first floor to keep me occupied." She wandered over to the large windows overlooking the gardens. Cold seeped through the glass. The window seat was huge. The cushion and pile of pillows beckoned her to climb in and dive into another world. Warmth from the fireplace to her left warmed her back. All she needed was a blanket to wrap up in, a cup of hot chocolate, and she could easily curl up all day reading as a fire crackled in the hearth. The only thing to make it picture perfect would be big, fluffy snowflakes.

With a sigh, she turned to stand in front of the fire. Ten people could stand in the hearth. The mantel was carved with flowers and leaves, a work of art in itself. She couldn't wait to see the rooms upstairs. Her room.

As if he'd read her mind, Featherton spoke. "Ready to see your chamber, Miss Smith?"

"Call me Elizabeth, please." With a last longing look at all the books, she followed Featherton upstairs, past several closed doors.

"The other rooms are currently under restoration, so please stay out of them for your own safety." He pointed to the door at the end of the hall. "The lord's chamber is locked and remains empty until he graces us with his presence."

"Does he visit often?"

A look crossed his face. "No. A distant relative owns the castle and has no use for an old pile of stones." He opened the door and stood back. "Your room."

The room was done in varying shades of pink. The hair on the back of her neck stood up the moment she crossed the threshold. The sensation of a malevolent presence made her touch the back of her neck, as if protecting herself from a blow. The cold, creepy feeling remained as she moved around the room, but she forced her mouth to curve into some semblance of a smile.

"It's very pretty. Do you and Martha live here at the castle?"

The dour look on his face softened. "We've been married almost forty years. Spent our honeymoon in Paris and then came here straight away. Our cottage lies at the edge of the woods. If you need anything, you only have to ring."

"I'm sure I'll be fine. I'm so excited to be here."

"I'll leave you to unpack." As he left the room, he turned to her. "Remember what I told you: do not enter the other chambers."

Her hand was in the pocket of her coat and she crossed her fingers when she replied, "I promise." Sunshine's voice filled her head. *Everyone knows if you cross your fingers when promising, it negates the promise.*

The driver had left her bags at the foot of the bed. The four-poster was piled high with pink floral pillows and thick blankets. A fire crackled in the fireplace, yet her unease lingered. The walls of the room were covered in a pale pink silk, and beautiful impressionist paintings hung on every wall. Her room had its own bathroom, which she assumed was a later remodel. It boasted a cast iron tub that sat under a window.

It didn't take long to unpack. She wandered around the room, looking at the pretty vases and trays scattered around on the tables. Elizabeth kept returning to the same spot to the right of the window seat. What had happened here? Cold hands pressed against her head. The sensation of being punched in the stomach made her fall to her knees. Doubled over, she gasped for breath even as she knew it was an illusion. When she could breathe again, she leaned against the wall, centering herself.

"There is nothing here. You haven't eaten enough today, that's all." She looked over her shoulder. "I don't believe in ghosts."

When she came down for dinner, the aroma wafting through the hall surprised her. It was odd sitting at a large table all by herself. Martha sang to herself as she brought the dishes out.

Seeing Elizabeth's look, the woman laughed. "I thought I'd make Italian for your first night with us. You'll be eating enough stews, soups, and potatoes the rest of the week." Martha's silver eyes sparkled in the candlelight. "Oh bother. I can't keep a secret at all. On Thursday you'll have a proper Thanksgiving feast. We wanted you to feel at home while you're staying here."

Elizabeth clapped her hands together. “I don’t know how to thank you. Thanksgiving is my favorite meal of the year.” She eyed the dishes. “These look really old. I’m almost afraid to eat off them.”

“Nonsense. As long as you don’t toss them at the walls, there’s nothing to worry about.”

“They’re beautiful.” The dishes had gold edges and a floral design around the rim. The pasta was calling her name. “So delicious. This sauce is to die for.”

“Eat up. You’re too skinny.”

“I won’t be if you feed me like this all week.”

Dinner consisted of fresh bread with olive oil for dipping, along with a side salad and a Chardonnay. The pasta was divine. Bowtie noodles in a cream sauce with chicken and spinach. Martha had done an outstanding job, and Elizabeth bet she’d gain five pounds this week. After dinner she made a beeline for the library.

Curled up with a book, she blinked when Featherton poked his head in the library. She had to reorient herself to this time and place.

“We’ll bid you a good night. If you need anything, ring.” He paused in the doorway. “Highworth creaks and groans when the wind blows, but don’t let it scare you. Old places have a life of their own.”

A nervous laugh escaped. “I felt the castle breathing earlier in my room.”

“We’ll see you in the morning. Breakfast at eight.” As he stood in the doorway, he looked down the hall toward the study. “Best not to wander about at night.”

With that nerve-racking statement, he left her alone. Elizabeth finished her tea and went back to reading the book she’d found tucked back on a shelf. It was an old book by an author she’d never heard of, some kind of mystery about a killer stalking stonemasons in Scotland. The cheesecake she’d enjoyed for dessert was fantastic, and she decided when she went back home, she’d drink tea every day.

When she kept rereading the same page over and over, Elizabeth decided she’d stayed up late enough to reset her internal clock. She closed the book, deciding she would finish it tomorrow. With every step up to her room, a yawn escaped.

The castle had been updated and boasted electricity and running water. She flipped lights off as she went, the darkness swallowing the space behind her. In her room, she still had the same unsettling feeling. And while technically she’d promised, she’d crossed her fingers, which in her book negated the promise. One quick look couldn’t do any harm.

Chapter Nine

Which room to snoop in first? Elizabeth started at the door closest to the stairs. Featherton telling her to stay out should have been enough, but in her mind he should have locked the room if he really didn't want her nosing about. The door swung open with a creak and she coughed, waving away the dust cloud. When she stepped into the empty room, a drop of water landed on her nose and she looked up to see a gaping hole in the roof. A cloud drifted by and moonlight filtered in, illuminating the stone floor. While it might be empty, this room, like hers, gave off a cold, creepy vibe.

"Well, that won't do at all."

The next room was also empty, though there was no hole in the ceiling and no scary feelings. A noise that sounded suspiciously like a squeak made her hurry out of the room, yanking the door shut.

"Nope. Not that one either."

There was one last room—the room Featherton said was locked. But it wouldn't hurt to try, would it? She stood in front of the door at the end of the hall, her hand poised above the handle. Wind blew across the stones, making the castle sigh, and she snatched her hand away, feeling like whatever she did next would irrevocably change her life. "Now you're being silly. It's only a room."

Grasping the handle, Elizabeth pressed down, bouncing on her toes when the door swung open without a creak. Cold stone met her fingers as she searched for a light switch like she'd seen in the rest of the rooms. It was too dark to see inside, so she went back to her room, lit a candle, and placed a glass globe over it to keep the flame from blowing out. The candlelight provided enough light to see a few feet ahead of her as she stepped into the room. The drapes were drawn, so the first thing she did was to pull them open, letting moonlight spill into the room.

"It's perfect. Absolutely perfect."

The hair on her arms and neck stayed put. Nothing made her feel like malevolent eyes tracked her every move, and, like Goldilocks, Elizabeth found this last room to be just right.

The walls were stone on two sides, the other two finished in deep blue, as if someone had updated half of the room, gotten bored, and left. The space oozed hedonism and masculinity. The bed had curtains at each corner, ready to shut the inhabitants inside a cozy nest, keeping out the biting cold. The expanse of bed made her itch to stretch out and see how far her fingers would be from the edges. While this room didn't have a bathroom, there was something about it that called out to her, tempting Elizabeth to sleep here tonight. The fireplace was empty. And as much as she wanted to, there was no way she could light a fire without giving away the fact she was snooping where she wasn't supposed to be.

"If I sneak back to my own room now, no one will ever know I was here." The room stayed quiet, waiting. Back in her own room, Elizabeth mussed up the bed so it would look like she'd spent the night. Book in hand, she padded back down the hall, into the welcoming room. As long as she removed all traces by morning, she thought she'd get away with sleeping here tonight. Tomorrow she'd try to stay in her assigned room, hoping the creepiness would move elsewhere.

The sound of thunder made her drop the book. Pressing her nose to the glass, she peered into the darkness. When lightning illuminated the grounds, she could see the storm clouds creeping closer, blotting out the moon. The next crash made her squeak. She jumped into the bed, pulling the covers up to her chin. They were soft, the linen worn smooth from years of use.

Between the cold and the storm, she was wide awake. A few chapters before bed would help ease the nervousness flooding through her body. The storm felt sinister as it crept closer and closer. Perhaps not the brightest idea to be reading a novel of psychological suspense before bed.

What if a crazed killer came out from a secret passage while she slept? “Rainbow Elizabeth Smith, now you’re being ridiculous.”

Saying it out loud helped. Losing herself to another time and place in a book would also help. After a few chapters, she had to go to the bathroom. Too much tea or nerves. The book landed on the floor as she slipped out from beneath the covers, and the cold made her flinch.

As she knelt down to pick up the book, the candlelight illuminated something under the bed. Her fingers touched a scrap of fabric. It felt like linen and was beautifully embroidered with flowers and vines. It also looked really old, like something she shouldn’t touch. Probably priceless. But it was a scrap with frayed edges. Maybe a ribbon at some time?

But she didn’t want to relinquish the piece. It comforted her. “Surely it won’t hurt to use it as a bookmark for one night?” Elizabeth knew she had a bad habit of talking to herself out loud whenever she was alone. Hearing the sound of her voice in the quiet made her feel less alone.

She hurried to the bathroom, wishing she'd brought slippers. A gust of wind blew down the hallway, extinguishing the candle. That was odd. The glass should have protected the flame, and she'd sworn all the doors and windows were shut. When she crossed the hall to check the room with the hole in the roof, Elizabeth tripped over the rug and went down hard on the stone.

"Ouch." Her knee burnt. Limping to her temporary room, she lit the candle again. The drops of blood welling up on her knee were the color of rubies in the warm light. A tissue stopped the worst, and she went back to the book.

Thunder rumbled and she slammed the book shut, the scary chapter not helping her overall mood. "Nope, no more creepiness tonight. Next time I'm going with a cotton candy romance." Yawning, she checked the time on her phone.

"Busy day tomorrow. Better get some sleep."

She turned on her side, and the crack of thunder was so loud the windows rattled. Elizabeth jolted up in bed, and her knee hit the nightstand, knocking the book to the floor. The lightning cast shadows in the room, and as she watched, they climbed the walls and oozed across the ceiling. As she picked the book up, the strip of fabric fell out, landing on her knee.

"Oh no. I've ruined it. With my luck it was probably worth thousands and thousands of dollars." Holding the linen to the candle, she gasped. Three spots of blood dotted the artifact. Her stomach flipped over. In the morning, she'd have to confess. Not only to breaking and entering but to ruining a piece of history. The look on Featherton's face would be one of disappointment. He'd politely ask her to leave, and she'd have to say goodbye to Highworth, all because curiosity once again got the better of her.

The windows crashed open, wind blowing through the room, sending the room into blackness. Elizabeth screamed, throwing the covers over her head, cowering, holding tight to the scrap of fabric.

The storm raged, and she knew if she didn't get out of bed and close the windows, everything in the room would be wet and ruined. "You can do this. Do it fast and get it done."

She jumped out of bed, blinking rain out of her eyes as she pushed against the wind to shut the windows. Water pooled on the floor dangerously close to the priceless rug. There was no time. Lightning flashed so close it left a jagged imprint on the back of her eyelids. No way no how was she leaving the safety of this room. The hallway would be dark, and her room... She shuddered. It would be even scarier. Elizabeth yanked the flannel nightgown over her head and mopped up the water on the floor. There was a hook on the wall near the fire. The gown would be dry in a few hours. Tonight she'd sleep in her birthday suit. Her creepy room needed the light of day before she'd venture back in there.

The windows rattled again and she leapt into bed, finding she was still holding tight to the scrap of fabric. The thought of cleaning it crossed her mind, saving her from telling Martha and Featherton what she had done. But what if it disintegrated? The lightning turned blue and green and she threw the covers over her head like a child. Underneath the thunder she heard the faint sound of music. Nope, she wasn't looking. What if there was a ghost in the room? This wasn't the kind of adventure she'd had in mind. She wanted fun, not a horror movie.

Elizabeth didn't know how long the storm raged before it finally settled down. Risking a peek, she peered into the blackness, unable to see anything but a few rough shapes. For a brief moment she swore the room seemed different. The smell of leather and wool and something spicy. But she chalked it up to nerves. As the adrenaline wore off, exhaustion set in and Elizabeth fell fast asleep.

Chapter Ten

Elizabeth woke to the sound of snoring. Snoring?

She shrieked. The body next to her pulled her close, throwing a rather hairy leg over hers. The body in question was a large man who reeked of alcohol and cheap perfume. He mumbled and touched her again, his hand stroking her breast, whispering what sounded like French into her hair.

The slap echoed across the room. "Take your filthy hands off me this instant."

The man sat up, bare-chested, with muscles in all the right places—not that she noticed.

"Didn't I pay you enough, demoiselle?" Bloodshot blue eyes roamed over her, making her snatch the blanket from the bed, wrapping it tightly around her.

"Why are you here? None of you are allowed to sleep

in my bed. And you know my rule: you are never to spend the night."

What a player. Steam came out of her ears, or at least she imagined it would if she were a cartoon. How dare he. "Pay me?"

"One does pay a whore for her services, yes? Or were your soft mewing sounds last night a gift?" He arched a brow, staring at her pale pink toes and leisurely making his way up to her face. "You are naked and in my bed, therefore you are a whore...or you are a reckless maiden seeking to trap me into marriage." He narrowed his eyes. "Know this: I care naught for your reputation. This is a mere trifle. Leave my chamber and go home to your sire."

Fury burnt through her. As she spluttered a scathing reply, a commotion sounded beyond the door. Great. Featherton was going to have her head. Right after she threw a fit. This room was supposed to be off limits. The lord of the castle never visited. Was it a prank?

The blood drained from her face, making her sway, dizzy for a moment. Oh, hell. Did this man own Highworth? He would make her leave, and she'd only arrived last night. No way—she wanted her full week here. Without him in what she'd decided was her room.

As the door slammed open, Elizabeth drew herself up to her full height. All five feet and five inches. Though it was a bit hard to look intimidating when you stood with a blanket wrapped around your naked body.

Several men and a boy barged into the room. The boy's mouth dropped open. "My lord, there's a faerie in your chamber."

The men with him crossed themselves.

"Look at her feet." One of the men pointed.

Another made a sign of horns with his fingers. "Begone, evil faerie."

The third man grabbed his hand and tried to whisper. "Do not. Look at her hair. She will curse us all."

Elizabeth barely resisted the urge to laugh.

"My lord. Er, you aren't wearing any clothes." The boy looked back and forth from her to the man in question.

Nice. Not only was he the owner, he'd brought a bunch of idiots with him. Elizabeth didn't find any of this a bit funny.

"Now that you mention it, Rabbie, she does look like a faerie." He made her a low bow. "My apologies. You are not a whore, you are a faerie." He tapped a finger to his lips. "Or are you a faerie whore come to take me away to the faerie hill?"

She made a face, instantly despising him. He sounded much too intrigued by the idea. Before she could retort, the sound of metal scraping against metal made her turn to find four swords pointed at her.

The tall man sniffed. "She smells nice. Best remove her before she curses all of us."

"Call me a whore one more time and I'll punch you."

She pointed at each man. “I’m not a faerie or a maiden. My name’s Elizabeth and this castle is mine for the week. What’s with the swords?” Elizabeth wrinkled her nose. “Bit over the top, don’t you think?”

This guy had serious delusions or a Renaissance faire fetish. But Elizabeth had to give them credit—the French they were speaking sounded surprisingly authentic. The bad words she recognized, but the rest was gibberish.

One of the men stepped forward. He must be the leader of these faux-knights. “Robert, she is no whore, nor is she faerie or witch. She is a lady, mayhap witless, and you have compromised her. Send a messenger to her father, telling him you will do right by the girl.”

The man called Robert scowled. “I woke to find her in my bed, unclothed. She most certainly is a whore.”

Elizabeth had had enough of being called a lady of the night. She hauled back to smack him again but he grabbed her arm, yanked her to him, and kissed her. The first thought that raced through her mind was he had a body made of marble. The second was how infuriating he was, and the third? Not one to lie to herself, she admitted he could kiss. The kiss started out demanding then turned questioning. She found herself responding before she came to her senses, pressed her palms to his bare chest, and shoved. Hard.

“She kisses like a whore.” He grunted and kissed her again, nibbling her lips. Time to teach the arrogant ass a lesson. Not to take without asking. She bit down on his lip.

The man swore and shoved her away.

"Take her to the dungeon until I'm ready to deal with this *lady* who claims to be neither whore nor faerie nor maiden." He glared at her, touching a finger to his lips. "As you do not enjoy my company, let us see how you prefer the rats."

The boy gasped. "My lord, they will eat her."

"Nonsense. Perhaps a few nibbles."

As the men took hold of her, she fought back, screaming at the top of her lungs, kicking and swearing. Her elbow connected with one of the men's noses. He dropped her, holding his nose as blood ran through his fingers.

"I will curse you if you don't release me this instant."

The others backed away, looks of terror on their faces. Except for the leader. He looked like he was holding in a laugh. And the man who'd accosted her? Robert? He looked furious, the intent plain on his face.

She made it three steps before her feet left the ground and she found herself looking at a very nice backside.

"I demand you put me down this instant."

The man who'd kissed her ignored her. No matter how much she twisted, kicking, screaming, and pounding on his back.

"You better have a fantastic lawyer. I'm going to have

you arrested for assault."

He jogged down the stone steps, making her head bounce against his back. Torches lit the way. Wait a minute. Torches? Had the power gone out? Or did he have such a gigantic ego, he demanded torches to give the castle an authentic feel? What an insufferable, heinous jerk.

Lifting her head to see where they were going made Elizabeth's neck ache, so she settled for looking to the side. Had he taken her through a different passage?

"Where are you taking me? Hello? This is so not funny."

He didn't answer. The hall looked different. But they passed through so fast she didn't have time to figure out what was bothering her. A man opened a door.

"My lord, might you reconsider? The lady can be placed in one of the other chambers until you decide her fate."

"Out of my way." He snarled at the man.

The guy gulped and moved. They were going down a set of stone stairs, the treads worn smooth in the middle. It grew colder and colder. Water trickled down the stone walls. At the bottom she saw rows and rows of casks.

A note of fear crept into her voice. "This isn't funny."

He kept moving, refusing to speak to her, bringing back the white-hot anger.

"Listen, you arrogant ass, put me down this instant."

Metal creaked, she caught a glimpse of bars, and the breath whooshed out of her as he tossed her to the ground. She landed on a pile of blankets, and a cloud of dust filled the air. Coughing and sputtering, Elizabeth managed to get to her feet. Not again. The cell door slammed shut and a key turned in the lock. He strode away.

"Wait. You can't just leave me here."

His boots slapped on the stone as he walked away from her. She heard him talking to the man who'd told him not to do this. Maybe he would help. "Hello? Tell him to let me go."

The men sounded like they were arguing.

"Damn you. I demand a phone call. I want my lawyer, you insane bastard." She threw in every curse word she knew, even inventing a few on the spot.

At that, he turned, came back, and peered through the bars, his blue eyes almost violet in the dim light from the torches. "Highworth belongs to me. The cheek of the lass."

The other man grinned. "By the saints, I've never heard such words from a lady."

"That's no lady."

Robert turned on his heel and left, the other man following.

Elizabeth stood there until the anger drained away. She sat down, careful not to send up another cloud of dust, and pulled the blanket tight around herself. She'd now been locked up eight times. But this was the first time she didn't have any clothes.

Chapter Eleven

Could it be? Were the fates laughing at him from above? Robert frowned. Punishing him for mocking them? The woman in his dungeon could only be one of two things: faerie or future girl.

If she was truly from the future, 'twas not her fault she woke in his bed. Did it mean Highworth stood through the ages to come? Was she mistress of the castle? He thought on her words. Nay, she said she was visiting for a sen'night.

Could she be a faerie? He had never seen such hair. Hers had long curls begging to be touched. But the colors? Purple, blue, and pink. Perhaps a faerie. If she was, she could not escape. His dungeon was made of iron, and all knew faeries could not abide iron.

Neither boded well. He could not afford distraction.

Had no time for her womanly matters. Not with Connor locked in the chamber upstairs, a price on his head. Nor with the guests arriving tonight.

"You should release her. Place her in the chamber next to Connor." Featherton finished buttoning the buttons of Robert's cotehardie. It fit snugly across the torso, and he raised his arms, checking the fit, ensuring it was not too tight to draw a sword. The rich velvet was embroidered with stags and other animals. The black pouch with the silver clasp was attached to the jeweled belt at his waist. Robert checked the weight.

"I added more gold, knowing who was in attendance tonight." His steward sniffed.

Robert grinned. "There will be many wagers. I intend to win them all." He looked down, pleased by his appearance. Lord Radford would be the only one dressed finer than he.

"I will see the wench, but mark my words, she is bound to bring trouble to Highworth."

Mayhap he should free her. Assist her in her quest to go home. But in truth, he did not know if she could travel back to her own time. Robert tried to remember what his brothers had told him. None of their wives had gone back, though he thought there was a chance they could... When everyone left and Connor was healed and gone, then he could see to the meddlesome female.

Until then, he would tell her nothing. What was one more lie of the hundreds he'd told women over the years? Future girls. They were always getting in the way. Robert could not let her cause trouble.

Robert's steward made a sound in the back of his throat indicating his disapproval as he left the chamber. After filling a cup with wine, Robert took the stairs down to the dungeon to check on his guest. As he approached the cell, he saw someone had found her a stool. She was sitting on it, leaning against the wall, staring into the distance. As he approached, she bolted to her feet, fists clenched at her sides.

"You look like a puffed-up peacock dressed like that. What is it, Halloween?" Even though she was shorter than him by eight inches, she managed to look down her nose at him. Robert's mouth twitched.

"What are you?"

"What am I?" She blinked at him. "I'm not a *what*. My name is Elizabeth Smith. I won the right to stay here for a week, and I don't find any of this the least bit funny, even if it is some kind of authentic castle experience." She stepped forward, gripping the bars so tightly her hands turned white. "Let. Me. Out. Now."

She was most definitely a future girl. "Where are your garments?"

"There was a storm. I didn't want the rug to get wet, so I cleaned up the rain with my gown." She mistook the look on his face for disapproval. Nay, he was most interested in her lack of a dress.

"I was the only one in the castle. Well, except for

Featherton and Martha, but they stay in a cottage at the edge of the woods."

He was so busy admiring her hair. It reminded him of the evening sky so much that he almost missed the words.

"You know Featherton?"

"Of course. He's the one who showed me to the chamber."

But she looked away and he knew she was lying. She squirmed, holding the blanket tight to her body. But how did she know his steward's name?

"Well, actually, he put me in the chamber down the hall. But it was creepy, so I went to the room at the other end of the hall. It was much more to my taste." She scowled at him. "If you are the owner, why are you here? It might be your room, but it's my castle for the whole week. So get out." Then she blinked at him, a look he'd seen on many a woman when they wanted his gold or his name.

"But first let me out so I can go back to sleep and wake up from this nightmare."

Robert rocked back on his heels. Tapped a finger to his lips as if thinking. "I am Robert Thornton, Lord of Highworth. No one had the authority to grant you the right to reside at my castle. And wenches are not allowed in my chamber. Ever. Nor are they allowed to spend the night. If I let you go, will you leave now and stop vexing me?"

Elizabeth put her hands on her hips and glared at him. He couldn't help but notice the pink in her cheeks, the fullness of her lips, and how her green eyes sparkled like emeralds when she was angry. Which she most definitely was. With him. 'Twas a new feeling. Wenches wanted him; they were never angry with him. Except when he left them.

"You listen to me. I'm not going anywhere. I won the week. I'm staying. For the full week."

"A wager? What was this wager granting you my home as the prize?"

"There was a contest. I wrote a letter explaining why I deserved to stay here for a week. I won. So Highworth is mine. You need to leave. Come back another week."

When he found out who'd wagered his home, he would take their head.

"It seems we are at an impasse, demoiselle. I will let you out when you pay the toll." He smirked at her.

"Toll?"

"A kiss."

"I wouldn't kiss you again if you were the last man on earth," she retorted.

"Such sweet words of wooing." Robert threw back his head and laughed. "You will beg me to kiss you, and perchance I might say aye."

"Never. I would rather kiss every pig in England than kiss you again."

"We shall see about that, Elizabeth Smith."

"Whatever." She infused the word with such disdain as she rolled her eyes. And with that one word, Robert knew with a certainty. This was no witch or faerie. This was a future girl. Saints, the wicked fates had heard his boast and sent her to vex him. No matter what he told Edward, this woman was not for him. Future girls were the downfall of two of his brothers and two of his friends.

He turned on his heel, walking away. Robert looked back, calling out over his shoulder, "As you will, Mistress Smith. I will have food and clothing sent down for you."

"Wait? Don't leave me down here."

He came back and stood in front of the bars. "Have you changed your mind? A kiss for your release?"

He watched as she narrowed her eyes and curled her lip. "I despise you. You are rude and arrogant. Nothing more than a misogynistic, hideous man."

While he might not have understood the meaning of all of her words, he certainly understood the tone. She was furious with him, and for the first time in a long time, ever since that dreadful night two years ago, Robert felt the weight of his choices lighten just the smallest bit.

"We will see if you feel the same after you spend a night in my dungeons." He left her bellowing at him, cursing like a hardened sailor from the docks.

Chapter Twelve

"Robert, you cannot leave her in the dungeon or treat her thus. You know whence she comes."

Not wanting any to overhear, he motioned Thomas into the solar. Robert paced in front of the fire.

"You and I both know future girls cause nothing but trouble. 'Tis a wonder my brothers survived. With Connor in the chamber above, 'tis not safe for any at Highworth. If he is found…I will be in the tower, my brothers stripped of land, title, and gold. And Mistress Elizabeth will find herself tied to a stake. You know how future women speak. The king's men will call her witch." He paced back and forth across the room, plotting.

"That is why you have treated her harshly. I knew you would not ill-use a woman. Will you send her to one of your brothers? Perhaps Edward?"

Robert stopped pacing. "Nay. Edward is putting down skirmishes and Henry and John have children."

"Christian would hide her."

He banged the cup down. "He would woo her."

"I thought you did not care for her shrewish tongue."

Robert heard the smile in Thomas' voice.

"She is not for Christian. I would not have him saddled with such a wench." Clenching his fists, he stomped across the room. "Radford. She will be safe with him."

Thomas looked horrified. "Saints, you cannot."

"He is in favor with the king. The man cannot resist a pretty face. I have heard tell he believes in faeries. He will think her one and hide her away. If I treat her harshly, he will believe it is because in truth I want her or I am afeared of her. He will do anything to have her, so I will wager on her and I will lose. He's always wanted to best me. Then he will take her and she will be safe with him. He is a lord, and honor bound to treat her kindly, as he would a prized horse."

Thomas snorted, hand on the sword at his hip. "I do not believe him to be an honorable man. But he would be a wise choice." He scratched his beard. "You cannot leave her with him overlong. There is something about the man I do not care for."

Robert resisted the urge to rub his hands together. "He will be so eager to best me, he will not wonder why I let a faerie go. Once Connor has healed and we have helped him escape England, then I will bring her back. She has a sharp tongue; by then he will be happy to be rid of our Elizabeth."

"Will you help her go back to her time? Send a messenger. Have one of your brother's wives come. They could talk to her, tell her what needs be done."

Robert snarled. "You know I cannot. What happened because of my carelessness."

Thomas shifted from foot to foot. "'Twas not your fault. You could not have known someone would take the information to the king. You could not have known they would kill those they found in the woods."

His captain put a hand on Robert's shoulder. "You must let go of the guilt. Tell John what happened. There is nothing to forgive, but he will forgive you. Your brothers must wonder why you have been absent of late."

Robert grimaced. "I cannot. Not while Connor is here. The risk is too great." He looked down, remembering when he'd found out what his careless words had wrought. "Mistress Elizabeth is a fine woman, but 'tis not safe for her at Highworth. For if any find out I am aiding Connor, I will be tried for treason and hanged. She would be all alone in this world with no family to care for her."

"I would see her to one of your brothers. They would aid her."

"Perchance you are right, Thomas. As much as it

pains me, we must play along with this ruse. Ensure Elizabeth thinks I despise her. Once Connor is safe and I fetch her back, then I will explain all."

Thomas pursed his lips. "Women are mercurial creatures. 'Tis not wise for her not to know what you are plotting. We should tell her. A future girl would understand your reasons."

Robert shook his head. "No. She must believe I cannot stand the sight of her."

"You care for her."

"Nay. I would aid her. See her back home. Nothing more."

Thomas raised a brow. "I will remind you of this when she's throwing her trencher at your head."

Did a man wait for her? The thought of another man possessing her made Robert see black.

Chapter Thirteen

If only Elizabeth hadn't opened the magazine, perhaps things would have turned out differently. Sunshine would bring over pizza and help her figure out what to do for a living. No more jail time, and under no circumstances of any kind would she find herself locked up in a dungeon of a castle. Especially while the infuriating owner pranced around as if he fancied himself some kind of medieval lord.

"This is an adventure. Find the fun." Her voice echoed on the stone as she remembered the advice her mom gave her whenever something didn't go well. "Hello? If there's a dragon down here, it would be fun if you'd turn Robert the conceited jerk into beef jerky."

Didn't dragons like gold? She didn't have any, but she could probably find Robert's stash and give it to the dragon in return for flying her out of here.

She kicked the pallet and watched the cloud of dust filter down through the dim light. There weren't any windows; the only light came from the torches around the walls. Torches. Why not electric lights down here? From everything she'd seen, the castle had been updated with electricity. Well, most of it. The chamber she'd snuck into didn't have a light switch. It was possible the owner hadn't gotten around to updating the basement. Or, more likely, this idiot had deluded himself into thinking he was living in the past.

When she shook the blanket covering her tiny bed, she sneezed. Even as a child she'd made her bed every day. Couldn't stand the sight of a wrinkle-rumpled mess. As she shook the blanket once more, a few twigs went flying and she heard a squeak. A mouse scurried through the bars to freedom.

"Wish I could fit through those."

Her voice was loud in the silence. She heard a soft chuckle from the man stationed near the stairway. He was the same guy who'd been there last night when Robert threw her in here. The guy coughed and pretended he hadn't laughed. Maybe he would help?

"Excuse me? You over there."

The man came toward her and she looked hard at him. The clothing he wore looked authentic. It must have cost a boatload. And his sword looked pointy and sharp. The first tremors of unease flowed through her, but she ruthlessly pushed them away.

"Mistress?"

"Can I get some water? And when am I getting out of here?"

The man scratched his ear. "Water? 'Tis not safe to drink. I will fetch you some ale." He cleared his throat. "You cannot leave. My lord says you are to stay and I am to guard you."

At least he left to fetch her something to drink. The man came back and handed her the cup of beer. He also handed her food in a wooden bowl. Some kind of stew and a chunk of bread. It was the bread that made her examine every moment from the time she'd woken to find Robert in her bed.

The bread had a few tiny pebbles in it. As far she knew, there was nowhere in England where she would expect to be served rocks in the bread. The man's speech was odd, and up close his clothing looked handmade. Maybe they had a seamstress on the payroll that made the clothing by hand?

"Thank you for the beer and food."

The man looked uncomfortable, averting his eyes from her. "Janet is bringing you something to wear." He went back to his post by the door, turning away from her. Her stomach growled, protesting no food for an entire day. During protests she'd gone without food for hours, and longer when she'd been arrested, but she liked three meals a day. The stew was delicious, even if the vegetables were a little mushy. Busy scraping the bowl, she didn't hear the young girl approach. The man who'd brought the food was with her.

He looked to Elizabeth. "Do not try to run. If you do, it will go badly for you."

When she moved to the far corner of the cell, he opened the door. The young girl had her arms full of clothing. The man was carrying what looked like a pair of leather shoes. He locked the door behind the girl.

"Janet does not speak."

The child watched her, not making any move to put the clothes down.

"I'm Elizabeth. Are those for me?"

The girl nodded.

"Thank you. It's hard keeping a blanket wrapped around you all the time."

The girl blushed. If she had to guess, Elizabeth would peg her at six or seven. What on earth had happened to her? She had the look of a trauma victim. The girl had black hair and brown eyes that were much too old for her.

Janet held up what looked like a nightgown or summer dress. The man coughed.

"'Tis a chemise. I will turn around while she assists you."

Elizabeth dropped the blanket. Growing up with her free-spirited parents, she'd learned at an early age not to be embarrassed by nudity. Janet helped Elizabeth into the chemise. It felt like linen, soft and worn, with tiny flowers around the neckline and hem. It must've taken someone forever to sew and embroider this by hand.

Next the girl helped her into one of the most beautiful dresses she'd ever seen. It was made out of wool, dyed a deep blue, and the embroidery was exquisite. Flowers and vines had been stitched around the neckline, sleeves, and hem. The dress was formfitting at the top, billowing out at the bottom. There were tons of buttons. No way she could undress herself. No zipper or pockets. The work that went into such a garment... She swayed. If this was all part of an elaborate joke, it had gone too far.

She smoothed her hands down the wool, grateful for the warmth. The girl fastened a cloak around her that was trimmed was some kind of fur. It too was wool, with intricate embroidery.

Janet held up a dark blue cloth and pointed at Elizabeth's hair. Then she touched it before snatching her hand back.

Before Elizabeth could hold it in, she burst out laughing. "I am not a faerie. I'm not here curse anyone, harm you, or take anyone under the hill to faerie land. All I want is to enjoy the rest of my week."

The girl looked dubious, but pinned up Elizabeth's hair. Then her small hands quickly laced the slightly pointed leather shoes.

Elizabeth's stomach plummeted down to her toes.

Was this some kind of scam? Had she gotten herself involved in a crazy cult? She put a hand on Janet's arm. "I'm just like you. Where I come from, people make their hair different colors." She paused and took a deep breath, being sure to pitch her voice low so the man guarding her wouldn't overhear.

"Are you here against your will, Janet?"

The girl shook her head. Elizabeth tried again.

"Do you have TV? Internet? A phone?"

The girl's eyes were huge as she shook her head again. The child flinched as Elizabeth kicked her makeshift bed.

"I'm so sorry. I didn't mean to scare you."

Just freaking great. This was definitely some kind of cult. "Don't be afraid of me. I'll find a way to get us both out of here."

The girl looked terrified as she banged on the door. The keys in the lock made Elizabeth jump. The girl ran out of the cell as if chased by some kind of movie monster.

When the door slammed shut, Elizabeth sat on the stool, thinking. Not only did she have to save herself, she had to find a way to save Janet. Who would've guessed the eccentric owner of the castle was running a cult? The contest must be the way they got women to come here. Once they were here, he locked them away. She had to escape before they sold her or did who knew what else to her.

Chapter Fourteen

"Janet. Did you see the faerie?"

The girl nodded.

Rabbie leaned close. "I've never met a faerie before, but Mistress Elizabeth seems rather tall for a faerie."

"Faeries can change so they look like us. She cannot be trusted." Joan nodded knowingly, and Robert suppressed a chuckle. He stepped into the kitchen.

"You helped her to dress?"

The girl nodded.

He knew he was being cruel. His mother would not have approved of how he was treating a woman. Both his parents had raised him to treat women with the utmost care, and now he had one locked in his dungeon. A future girl who, through no fault of her own, had ended up at Highworth. When he explained all, she would laugh. He hoped she would.

"Rabbie, make sure no one goes down to the cellar."

The boy bobbed his head. Joan hurried off and Robert caught Rabbie looking after her with longing eyes.

"You know you can always live with John at Blackmoor."

The boy sighed. "Nay. When I spoke to him, he gave me his blessing to serve you. I miss him and the others, but I cannot leave Joan." The wistful look on his face made Robert wish he could tell the boy there would be many women in his life, but instead he offered aid.

"As much as it would pain me to lose you and Joan, if you would prefer to serve John, I will send her with you to Blackmoor."

The boy looked as if he were considering the offer, but Robert hoped he would not go. For he had become fond of the boy over the past few years, grateful John had sent him to Highworth that dark day.

"Joan has family in the village. We will stay here."

"As you wish. Now run along and make sure no one finds our guest."

Robert heard a commotion in the great hall, the sound of voices. There he found Featherton greeting his guests. Robert spoke to two of the men, who always brought fine horses with them. Then he stepped outside to meet the rest. Carriages and horses filled the courtyard. Stable boys scampered about. The men, other third and fourth sons like him, richly dressed and eager to spend a few days enjoying themselves, departed from the carriages.

As he counted his guests, the most ornate carriage of all rolled to a stop. He knew it well. It was Paul, Lord Radford. The man spent more time at court than he did at his own estates. Always trying to curry favor with the king, he would be first in line to inform their sire that Robert was giving shelter to a wanted man.

"Radford. Welcome to Highworth."

The man looked around as he descended from the carriage making a face as if he smelled something dead. "'Tis smaller than I remembered."

Robert knew it was going to be a trying few days, but refrained from saying so. "If you follow me, Featherton will see you settled in the best chamber."

"I hope you have found quality wenches for the festivities. Not those slovenly tavern wenches from the village."

"I believe you will be quite satisfied."

Robert greeted the rest of the guests and made sure the servants provided wine to all in attendance. Once everyone was inside the hall, he gave the order for the feast to begin.

Platters piled high with mutton, stag, pheasant, and rabbit were placed on the tables, along with bread, cheeses, carrots, and winter squash. Musicians played, and Robert was gratified to see the envy on Radford's face. He had paid dearly for them to be here for the next sen'night. Though he hoped, if all went well, his guests would be gone in a day or so. Robert planned to spread a rumor that there was illness. Nothing drove nobles away as quickly as the thought of becoming ill.

"The wenches will attend us after supper. We will play chess and wager."

One of the men raised a cup. "Horse racing tomorrow."

Another man halfway down the table raised his. "My horses are faster. I plan to depart with your gold."

They laughed, and Robert nodded at the servants to bring in the next course and more wine.

Featherton leaned down close to his ear. "The wenches have arrived. Shall I have them brought in?" He sniffed, the disapproval evident in his tone.

"Give them ale and bring them in."

The men banged their cups on the table as the women entered the hall. They were all shapes and sizes, something to please every man in attendance. Robert had gone to great expense to ensure his guests' pleasure. Some of the women pulled the men to the center of the hall to dance. Servants cleared the tables, pushing the benches and tables to the sides of the hall. Several would be left near the fire for those who wished to play chess.

'Twas as good a time as any to check on his guest. Robert slipped away from the hall and up the stairs, nodding to the guard on duty.

Connor opened his eyes and groaned as he struggled to sit up.

“I hear music. Ye know ’tis not wise. If anyone finds me here, will be both our heads.”

Robert poured the man a glass of wine. “Did you drink the healer’s foul brew tonight?”

The Scot grimaced. “Aye. Only to keep the wee lassie from weeping.” He sat up, breathing heavily from the effort. “Foul-tasting potion.”

Robert raised a cup. “I could not send everyone away; would raise too many questions. I have guards posted, and if anyone asks, I will say the chamber is under repair and unsafe. As long as you are quiet and don’t call out like a woman, all will be well.”

“When I am able, we will cross swords in the lists and then we shall see how free you are with your slurs, ye wee bastard.”

Robert laughed. “I shall look forward to it.” He told Connor about the guests in attendance and saw the worry in the man’s eyes.

“Radford will not hesitate to give us up to the king. Anything to better his station.”

“Leave him to me. I will do my best to see them gone in a few days.”

The Scot frowned. “Do not tempt the fates. Send them away on the morrow.”

“As soon as I can.” Robert sat back, talking to the

man as they discussed the best course of action. Rancor swirled through him that he must give up his revelry because of a debt he owed. Was it not bad enough he had a future girl locked in his dungeons? What was next? Robert shuddered and wished he had not asked the question. For he knew the fates were not done tormenting him yet.

Chapter Fifteen

Elizabeth had pried at every corner, wiggled every bar, and found no way to escape. A bribe came to mind, but without money or anything else of value to offer, well, it wasn't like a smile was going to do her much good. She'd learned that from her previous seven stays in the poky.

While she'd been locked away down here, she'd decided there was no way this was a prank. If it had only been a few hours she might have believed so. But now? Now all she could think was that something else was going on. With nothing but time on her hands, she'd gone over every moment since she'd arrived in England. The only thing that stood out was the terrible storm. What had happened to the beautiful strip of fabric? Looking down at her dress, she decided it was indeed a scrap meant for the rag bin. She'd gone to sleep, afraid of the storm and then woken to snoring. *Him.* Finding Robert the jerk in her bed. Of course, he'd claimed was his bed and she was the interloper.

There didn't seem to be any kind of rational explanation except for the whole cult idea. "A cult of medieval re-enactors." Sounded crazy when she said it out loud. As she sat pondering her situation, Elizabeth heard voices. A man entered the dungeon. The guard had tried unsuccessfully to keep him from coming further into the room. She stood, hoping perhaps this man could help her.

"Hello? I'm over here." She waved her hands through the bars to catch his attention. He swayed on his feet and changed direction, staggering toward her.

He made a clumsy bow. No doubt some hedge fund guy who liked playing with fake swords on the weekends.

"Lord Radford, at your service, lady." He peered into the gloom and sniffed. "Why is such a beauty locked away?"

Not one to ignore a chance at freedom when it presented itself, Elizabeth put on her most charming smile. The man in front of her was short and squat. He smelled of body odor and wine. The guy was dressed even fancier than Robert. He must have a lot of money and clout by the way the guard was acting.

"Robert...Lord Highworth and I had a disagreement. He locked me up." She batted her eyelashes. "Surely one as powerful as you can help me. I would be most grateful. Would you set me free?"

The man looked to be approximately five feet tall. He puffed up to his full height, and Elizabeth noticed he was wearing some kind of buckled shoe with what looked like a heel on it. He had skinny legs encased in yellow hose and he wore a longer jacket than Robert did. It was yellow and brown. Formfitting and buttoned—maybe silk? It looked like there were actual jewels sewn onto the fabric, winking in the dim light. Who were these people?

The man imperiously waved a hand at the guard. "Release the lady at once."

The guard spluttered, hemming and hawing before the guy called Lord Radford stamped his little foot.

"Do you dare to disobey my order? You know who I am. Release the lady. At once."

The guard's face turned bright red, making her feel the tiniest bit sorry for him. The man walked over slowly as if going to death row. Muttering to himself, he turned the key, opening the door. Without waiting for him to move, Elizabeth pushed past him and touched the good samaritan on the arm.

"I don't know how to thank you. I didn't think I would ever get out of here." As she moved past him, he grabbed her arm.

"Not so fast, lady. There are many men upstairs. You must allow me to escort you for your own safety."

"That's very nice of you." She took his arm and let him lead her up the stairs. As they walked into the great hall, she blinked, her mouth falling open. It was the same room and yet it wasn't.

There were men drinking and women in various states of undress scattered around the hall. Musicians played as she scanned the room looking for Robert. The hall looked newer than when she'd arrived. The tapestries brighter, the tiles on the floor a deeper color. Almost as if she were in a newer version of the exact same hall. As she looked around, her knees shook and her mouth went dry. All of the men were dressed alike. And the women. They wore simpler dresses than she did. They were obviously what Robert called a wench or what she would've called a hooker. And there were the torches again. No electricity in evidence. Anywhere.

As Elizabeth stood there pondering exactly what had happened to her, Robert appeared, stalking across the room. Somehow she resisted the urge to break free and run.

"Highworth. Look what I found when I went in search of the good wine you always hide away." Lord Radford waved an arm at her, and she noticed the other men paying attention to them and their conversation.

The look on Robert's face was priceless. His left eye twitched, which she'd noticed always happened when he was being an ass. Tension radiated from his body. She'd seen the same rigid stance in men before they brawled.

Unconsciously, she took a step back, waiting to see what would happen. She looked around, but there were too many men with hands near their swords for her to make a run for it. And the swords. What was up with all the swords? They didn't look fake.

"She is my prisoner. You should not have released her without speaking with me."

It was the wrong thing to say. The little man puffed himself up. "Your prisoner. Does she not belong to the king, as do all in the realm?"

Robert clenched his teeth together and Radford smiled, an oily smile. For the first time since he'd released her, Elizabeth thought she might have made a colossal mistake. What if this Lord Radford was worse than Robert?

The little man looked her up and down, making Elizabeth feel like she was back wearing a blanket with nothing underneath it.

"I will take her with me so you will no longer have to bear her presence. I will see that she gets to the king. He can decide what to do with her."

Robert looked to her, searching her face, and she tried to convey a message back. Only she didn't know herself if she wanted to go with the little man or stay. All she knew was that as soon as she could, she was making a run for it. All the way back to London and a nice, normal hotel.

Robert narrowed his eyes at Radford, then smiled.

"The king is busy; we should not bother him with such a trivial matter. Let us settle this matter with a wager, what say you?"

There were shouts from around the room. Other men moved closer, walking around and looking at her like she was a horse for sale at auction. The little man examined his nails, flicking his fingers when he looked up at Robert.

"A wager indeed. The winner takes the lady."

Elizabeth felt her mouth fall open. The nerve. She wasn't an object. They couldn't bet on her. What kind of crazy had she fallen into? As she opened her mouth to disagree, she caught Robert's look and snapped it shut. There was something else going on here, something she didn't understand. She took a deep breath. Could she trust him? He'd been nothing but awful to her from the moment she'd woken up. Yet this little man, there was something about him—a meanness around his eyes that made her nervous. Until she could escape and go to the police, she decided she'd play along.

Other men called out suggestions. The wenches walked around, looking at her. Some of them sniffing, others making comments.

"Look at her, she's far too skinny," one of the women said.

Another peered closely at her. "But look at her skin. Like a babe."

One of the knights came close, and Elizabeth had to

breathe through her mouth, he smelled so awful. “I would wager for the wench.”

Radford huffed. “The wager for the woman is between Highworth and me.” He frowned at the man. “There are plenty of wenches here for you; go find one.”

The man grumbled but left them alone. Elizabeth shivered even though fires roared in all six fireplaces. Robert walked around, looking her up and down from head to toe.

“Let us get on with it. She isn’t much to look at, and she has a tongue that will make your ears bleed. I want to drink and find a woman to warm my bed this night.” He let out a long-suffering sigh, as if she were a puddle of something spilled on one of his precious rugs.

“Nay, she isn’t worth very much,” he said.

Elizabeth resisted the urge to reach out and punch him. Robert stepped back, sensing the violence in her. Smart man.

Radford looked her up and down. “What did you have in mind?”

Robert smiled, the grin of a con man. “I saw you brought your two best horses. Add the horses and a bag of gold and then I might be inclined to wager.”

The short man belched, not bothering to cover his mouth. “I know you, Highworth. You would not ask for so much if she were worth so little. First we wager for the girl. Once you lose, I will allow you another chance to win her back. Then I will pledge my horses. And you will add all the wine in your cellar. Do we have an accord?"

Robert held out his hand. "We do. Shall we begin?"

She was being auctioned off. Like she was nothing more than a piece of property, these arrogant men were deciding who would get to claim her. She was loath to admit it, but her feelings were hurt. What had she done for Robert to be so mean to her? Was it all because she'd slapped him for trying to take advantage of her? If so, he was a world-class jerk. To say such awful things about her. She despised him.

A cold clarity swept through her. This was no cult. She pushed the thought away just as quickly. There was no way it could be true. It couldn't be, could it?

Elizabeth had never been one for fairytales. Never read romance novels. She was too busy trying to save the world. When she was eight, she'd set up a lemonade stand to raise money to free a wolf that was on display in a run-down shopping center. She freed the wolf and the activism bug had bitten her hard. Her parents were so proud of her that they'd encouraged the behavior through the years.

Why hadn't she paid more attention to history? She was always too busy figuring out what needed to be fixed. Like better lunches or higher pay for teachers. What use was the past? It sure would come in handy right now. Because no matter how much Elizabeth tried to deny it, somehow she'd fallen through time. The only question was—*when* was she in England?

Chapter Sixteen

As Elizabeth stood there gaping, coming to terms with the fact she was somehow in the living, breathing past, some kind of dice game was taking place. She heard one of the men call it "hazard."

Robert and Lord Radford were seated at a table in front of the fire in comfortable chairs. There was wine on the table, and one of the men pushed her down roughly onto the low stool across from them, like a particularly ugly vase up for auction.

Men gathered round to watch as all boasted how good they were, if only they could play too.

"Play your own games," Lord Radford said to the men. There were two dice, and she watched, trying to figure out the game as Lord Radford threw them. Men quickly placed bets, wagering on whether he would win or lose. It seemed to go back and forth for a while. She couldn't really follow it, but then she heard a cheer and realized Robert had won.

He smirked at her. "Told you I would win, Mistress Smith."

Lord Radford looked furious. He drank deeply, setting the cup down with a bang. "I will add my best horses for another game. We race at dawn."

Robert leaned back in his chair and Elizabeth somehow resisted the urge to stick out her foot and catch the leg, tripping him. The man was insufferable. He raised a cup to his opponent.

"'Twill be my pleasure to best you, Radford." He stood up, bowing to all in attendance as men exchanged money based on who had won the wagers.

"On the morrow."

While everyone was otherwise occupied, Elizabeth edged out of the room. Halfway across the hall, she flinched when Robert's captain stood in front of her.

"Going somewhere?"

"Thomas, right?"

He nodded.

"I'm leaving. I have had enough of this insane asylum."

His mouth twitched as he looked to where Robert stood. "I cannot let you leave. I will escort you to your chamber."

She shot a glance at him. "Are you taking me back to

that awful jail cell?"

"Nay, lady. I am taking you to your chamber. You are a guest at Highworth." He held out his arm, and she had no choice but to take it. She'd bide her time. Tomorrow while they were racing she'd have another opportunity to try to escape.

He led her up the stairs, and she had a moment of déjà vu so strong she put a hand on the wall to steady herself. Was it only a few nights ago she'd walked down this very corridor as she followed Featherton to her chamber? The Featherton now must be the present-day Featherton's ancestor. Wait until she told him what happened. Were he and Martha frantically searching the castle looking for her at this very moment? If only she could find a way to let them know she was trapped in time.

What would've happened if she'd stayed in her own room? If she hadn't been creeped out and opened the door to what she now knew was Robert's chamber? Would she still be in her own time?

He opened a door and she blinked. It was the chamber she had initially been given. When Elizabeth walked in and looked around, she noticed the furnishings were the same but the decorations were different.

The walls were painted pale yellow and there was a rug on the floor. None of the awful pink from when she stayed there. There was a pretty ewer and basin on a small table next to the bed. She sat on the bed, running her hands over the bedspread. It felt like wool, as did the blankets. The sheets were soft and there was a feather mattress and pillows. Sumptuous for any time. The room didn't feel creepy now. When had the creepy vibe taken over the space?

"How did you come to Highworth? None of my men saw you arrive." Thomas fidgeted.

What to tell him? She couldn't exactly say she'd gone to sleep in the future and woken up in the past. He was watching her so closely that for an instant she had the feeling he knew. But that was ridiculous.

"When I arrived, no one was here but Featherton."

Thomas frowned. "Yet he did not see you arrive."

She shrugged. "It's strange, isn't it?"

"Indeed." He looked as if he wanted to say more, but when nothing came out of his mouth, she moved to look out the window.

"Someone will come for you in the morning."

"Wait."

He turned and looked at her.

"What if I have to go to the bathroom?"

He blinked at her for a moment, and then his face brightened as if he'd understood her words. "This way." He motioned to a small alcove off the room.

Elizabeth made a face. He mistook the look for one of interest. Thomas stood next to her and pointed. "'Tis the latest garderobe. See, the seat is covered with cloth.

The…er…waste…falls down the chute into a barrel, which is emptied every day."

He pointed to a pile of rags. "There is wool and linen to…take care of…wipe…yourself. Along with a basin and jug of water to wash when you're done."

The burly man's face was as red as his hair by the time he finished talking. She had to bite the inside of her cheek so she wouldn't laugh. As he left, she heard the key turn in the lock. Locked in. Exchanging one prison cell for another. At least they'd left her wine to drink. She'd never drunk so much alcohol as she had since landing in the past. The water must not be good, or everyone here thought it wasn't good. Elizabeth stopped, remembering very few people drank water unless they knew it was clean. She felt a little bit dehydrated and looked down, feeling like the skin on her hands looked wrinkled, and she imagined her face looked the same.

She was unsure of the year, but pretty certain she'd landed in medieval England. Oh hell no—it better not be during the plague. Before she worked herself up into a state, Elizabeth decided if the plague was happening, people would be talking about it. So was it before or after?

There was no way she was going to be able to get out of the dress by herself. She walked around the room looking at everything, but there was nothing she could find to use as a weapon or to help her escape. With a sigh, she sat in the alcove by the window and leaned her head against the yellow wall. She thought she must've dozed off when she heard the lock turn and a woman came bustling in.

"I'm Joan, here to help you prepare for bed, mistress."

"Thank you. I tried but couldn't undress by myself."

The girl smiled and helped Elizabeth undress. She held up the dress, looking it over with a critical eye. "I will clean the stain off the bottom and be back in the morning to help you dress. Is there anything else you require before I leave?"

"Yes, I want to go home. How about you let me slip out the door? No one will know."

The girl looked horrified. "Nay, I cannot. Lord Highworth has been good to me. He took me in when I was starving. Found a place for my family in the village. I cannot go against him. He has been kind to me. To all of us here."

Elizabeth recognized unwavering loyalty when she saw it. Nothing she said was going to sway her. So she simply nodded. "Thank you for helping me undress. I'll see you in the morning."

The girl left her standing there in her chemise. From the voices, it sounded like there was a guard stationed outside of the door. Thomas had stoked the fire, but it was cold in the room. Climbing into bed, she was restless. And after a while, she swore she heard a noise.

Pressing her ear against the wooden door, she strained to hear. A door opened and she heard voices. Not English voices, but what she could have sworn was a Scottish accent. She hadn't heard one since she'd arrived and knew she hadn't heard the distinctive accent in the hall earlier. Who was the mystery guest?

Chapter Seventeen

Robert woke to a darkened room, still seeing the faces that haunted his dreams. He knew there would be no more sleep tonight. After pouring a cup of wine, he sat in front of the fire, staring into the flames.

Thomas was right. He could not have known the outcome of his actions. The knowledge did not excuse the carelessness. It had been more than two years since his brother John was returned to the living. When he and his brothers found out John was not dead, but had in fact been living as the infamous bandit of the wood, preying on the rich and giving to the poor, Robert had been overjoyed.

How had time passed so quickly? Robert had been visiting an estate on the coast. There had been hunting and wagering. Drinking and wenching. All of his favorite things. One night, deep in his cups, one of the nobles asked about John. Of what it must have been like to know he was the bandit of the wood. There was grumbling from the nobles who had been relieved of gold and horses at his brother's hands. The king had pardoned John after a stay in the tower, thanks to Anna. The woman from the future had stood beside his brother, made a life with him.

And being the center of attention, everyone waiting to hear what he knew, Robert boasted. Spoke of all the men, women, and children that had found sanctuary in a small keep on the coast near Scotland. How a few at a time would slip out, making their way to John to find sanctuary behind the walls of Blackmoor Castle.

Robert refilled his cup. So many dead because he could not keep his mouth shut. There had been a woman. He pressed his lips together. There was always a woman. And the night he bedded her, she had told him of the camp. And the keep where she now lived. Like a child with a new sword, he had boasted to all present.

Then, six months ago, Robert found out the price of his actions. The information he shared had been used to slaughter men, women, and children. Nay, not all of them were innocent. But all had gone to the woods looking for sanctuary his brother provided. And when the camp had fallen, they found it again in the keep. Until Robert destroyed them.

The king's men had hunted them down and killed them. And at another hunting party, the man who had taken the information to court boasted of the outcome. Robert had gone cold upon hearing the news. Guilt festered within him ever since. And he had pushed his family away. Not wanting to see his brothers, afraid they would see the knowledge of the mistake in his eyes. How could he ever look John in the eye again? Tell his brother the people he had tried to keep safe were dead because of Robert?

So he had done the only thing he knew how: pushed everyone away and lost himself in drink and ribaldry. Knowing at some point he must tell John what he had done but unwilling to face his brother. And by not being able to tell John, he could not see Edward or Christian or Henry. For they would be disappointed in him. The terrible consequences of his actions would be forever reflected in their faces. So he hid away at Highworth, making excuses. And he could've gone on this way for some time, until Elizabeth appeared in his bed.

He pressed his lips together, remembering the scent of roses. Feeling soft skin next to his and for an instant thinking his wife was beside him in his chamber. A snort escaped. She had been most displeased when he had pulled her close, nuzzling her ear. Her green eyes flashing in anger. The hair the color of the dying sun making him long to wrap each curl around his finger.

Knowing what he did about whence she came, he

could not blame her. For somehow she had gone to sleep in her time at Highworth and woken in his bed in the past. It was a small comfort to know his home still stood in the future. What year did she come from? How did it work, the traveling through time? He had heard Anna tell the story, but still wasn't sure what he believed.

When he retrieved Elizabeth from Radford, he knew he was honor bound to tell her why he had done what he had. Let her know there were those here who might be able to help her. Though her sharp tongue and lively wit would be sorely missed. She had only been here a few days and already he had grown accustomed to her presence. Seeking out her face if only to hear her bellow at him. And now he would have to send her away for a short time. Only to bring her back to Highworth and then find a way to send her to her own time.

Robert did not want Elizabeth to leave. The fates must be laughing at him. He had tempted them one too many times, and this was to be his punishment. To find himself wanting to be close to Elizabeth yet knowing he could not make her his lady.

As the winter sun rose in the sky, the darkness banished by the light, Robert stood and stretched. No matter how much it galled him to lose to Radford, he would do it to keep her safe.

Chapter Eighteen

Warm under the covers, Elizabeth stuck her foot out, testing the temperature. The cold made her dread getting out of bed. Weak sunlight filtered in through the window, casting stripes across her hands. The chemise today had vegetables embroidered all around the neck and hem in a soft pink thread. It was a different feeling, not wearing undergarments. For the first time since puberty, Elizabeth was happy to belong to the small-chested gals club.

Joan bustled into the room. "I brought ye a cup of wine."

With a groan she slid out of bed, wiggling her toes when they touched the cold stone. The girl had laid out the blue dress minus one suspicious stain on the hem.

"Where do you come from?" Joan stretched out a

curl as she brushed Elizabeth's hair.

"A place called Kentucky. It's very far away."

"I've never heard of it." Joan hummed as she worked to pin Elizabeth's hair up in an elaborate design. She wondered why the girl bothered, since it would be covered up anyway.

"Do all ladies have such hair in your land?"

She thought of all the interesting hair colors she'd seen at home. "A few. My real hair color is brown, like yours. Where I come from, most women color their hair."

The embroidered cloth now hiding her hair helped keep her head warm, so at least there was that.

"Why do you change your hair?"

"It's fun." She turned to smile up at the girl. "What do you do for fun?"

Before Joan could answer, the door swung open and Robert strode in. Of course he didn't knock. Everything about the man irritated her. From the way he stalked across the room, to the rich timbre of his voice. He glanced at her with a critical eye, as if he somehow found her lacking. While she wasn't full of herself, Elizabeth knew men found her attractive. So why did he persist in pushing her away? It was almost as if he was purposely trying to make her hate him. But why? *Men.*

"Is she ready?"

"Aye."

Joan scrambled to her feet, scurrying out of the room

as if the devil himself was after her. Though in this case the devil's name was Mr. Rude. Otherwise known as Robert, Lord Highworth. A small giggle escaped as Elizabeth almost called him Lord High and Mighty. Talk about being full of oneself.

"The lady is amused?"

She smiled sweetly. "By your face."

He blinked, unsure if she was insulting him or not.

"I heard voices last night outside my door. Maybe you should rename the place Highworth Prison."

He gave her sharp look. "One of my men."

"No. This wasn't an English voice. He sounded Scottish."

Robert took a step closer to her, sucking all the oxygen out of the room. While he was rude and arrogant, she had to admit he certainly had the movie star looks down pat. The man could easily grace a Sexiest Man Alive magazine cover. With sun-kissed blond hair and piercing blue eyes, his outer shell was enough to make her swoon. But the fact that he was such a pig kept her upright and immune to the megawatt smile.

"You are mistaken, mistress. You are the only guest who plagues me so. Besides, we are at war with Scotland. Any Scot found in the castle would be put to death. While I would likely be charged with treason." He looked down, fiddling with the sword at his hip.

She looked at the belt he was wearing. The amount of

jewels on the belt would provide lunch for a great many low-income children for a year or two. Who was this guy?

"There are rats in the castle. I'm sure 'tis what you heard last night. Best stay in your chamber so you aren't bitten."

"Like the mythical monster rats in the dungeon?" She gave him her best fake yawn. "Whatever helps you sleep at night." Elizabeth spotted a smudge of dirt on her forearm. She'd tried to wash the best she could with the rag and basin but must have missed a few spots. The thought of a hot shower made her close her eyes, imagining the heat easing sore muscles. "Any chance I could have a bath? I didn't see a tub in the bathroom... er...garderobe."

"There is no time. Come along. I must win the final two wagers to keep you here at Highworth. Though in truth, I should forfeit and be done with you, troublesome lass."

"These stupid wagers are all your fault. I'm done with you and England. Where I come from, you cannot wager a person. Let me leave so I can go home."

"'Tis not possible. And you are not in your country; you are in mine. Here you are worth as much to me as a cow. Lord Radford has taken an interest in you. He is a powerful noble with the ear of the king."

"Did you call me a cow?" Before she exploded, Elizabeth consciously unclenched her fists and took several deep breaths. She'd learned during the years of protesting how to pick her battles. This wasn't the time or the place to fight with him. She would wait and find another time. Because one thing she knew...no matter what, she was getting back to her own time and leaving this awful place. Wait until she told Sunshine and Darla what had happened to her. Never again would Sunshine ooh and ahh over a knight from another time. It wasn't romantic and nice in the past; it was filthy, unsafe, and horrible. *But it could be nice. Especially if a certain pig decided to be kind.*

Shut up, she told the voice in her head.

He opened the door. "Cows do not speak." The man in the corridor stood to attention as Robert looked her over, tapping his lip. "Nay, I would say you are like a fisherman's wife, always vexing me."

"And you are a slimy slug that crawls around the outside of a trash can." She took his arm. "I'm famished. Since I can't have a bath, tell me you at least provide breakfast for the prisoners."

He turned that million-dollar smile on her. "I would never starve such a beauty. I am not a barbarian."

"Could have fooled me."

In the hall, he led her to a seat in the middle of one of the tables. The bowl in front of her looked and smelled like oatmeal. One of the men saw her sniffing.

"'Tis porridge."

"Smells good."

He grunted and dug in. There was dried fruit, butter, and cream provided to add to the food. She ate, hungry and grateful for the filling meal. There was wine or ale, so she went with the wine. At least it would warm her up. Ever since she'd woken up in the past, she'd been cold. Elizabeth had felt silly wearing the cloak inside, but here in the hall, seated away from the fire, she was grateful and didn't care who looked at her funny. She pulled the cloak tighter, wishing for a nice, chunky scarf and gloves, or better yet, electric heat. With it this cold inside, she dreaded to think what it must be like outside.

"Come with me, mistress. We'll go up to the battlements where we can see everything." Rabbie offered his arm.

Elizabeth brought the cup of wine with her. It wasn't hot chocolate, but it would have to do.

"Lead on." The winding steps took them to the very top of the castle.

"The view is spectacular."

Forest and land, occasionally dotted with small houses, lay before her. No commercial development of any kind. The lack of strip malls was a plus for being in the past. Rabbie sat on the wall, his legs dangling over the edge. She peered over, watching everyone coming and going, the men gathering around as Robert and the frog, as she had come to call Lord Radford after their meeting, prepared to find out who was the better man.

While she looked around, what was wrong with the

entire scene finally hit home. While her mind told her she had fallen through time, it was difficult to believe. But looking out over the grounds—there was no paved parking area outside of the castle. No paved roads. No cars. She stood still, listening.

Over the sounds of metal, voices, and animals, she heard nothing but the wind. No modern-day noises. No cars, no horns, no planes in the sky. Not a single ringing cell phone. She'd kept trying to convince herself she truly had landed in the past, but it was the lack of the roads that finally convinced her beyond any doubt. Rabbie caught her arm as she swayed.

"Take care, mistress. My lord would not be pleased if you fell over the edge." He looked over. "Your head would split open like a melon."

Boys. Bloodthirsty, no matter the century.

"Thank you for looking after me." Stepping back, Elizabeth racked her brain. Finding herself trapped in the past meant she needed to know everything she could about this time.

"Excuse me. What's the date today?" She'd been too afraid of the answer before to ask. Now, accepting she was here, Elizabeth needed to know.

The boy shrugged, more interested in what was going on below. The guard passing by spoke slowly as if she were a rather stupid child.

"'Tis Wednesday, the thirteenth of November."

"And what is the year?"

The knight and the boy blinked at her, the guard taking a step back, like she had escaped from the funny farm and he wasn't sure what her next move might be. The man looked over the wall, down at the men assembled below, before looking at her.

"It is the Year of Our Lord 1333."

She clenched the cup and took a deep gulp, draining the red wine. "Thank you. I guess I forgot."

They looked unconvinced, but let it go as a shout rose up, drawing their attention. The men were on their horses, the excitement in their voices rising up as they called out, making their choice for the winner. Men shouted, horses' hooves thundered, and Elizabeth barely paid attention, still stuck on the date. It was 1333. A very long time from 2016. She'd guessed she'd landed in medieval England, but to hear the date out loud, so many things now made sense. Castigating herself for not paying more attention during history or taking an interest in world news, Elizabeth opened every file cabinet in her brain and rifled through the contents, looking for any scrap of information she might have stored away regarding this time period.

As she was sifting through various tidbits, a shout filled the air. She looked down to see the frog had won the horse race. Robert's voice carried, clear and deep.

"We have each won a wager, therefore we shall have a third to decide the winner. Would you agree, Radford?"

The man puffed himself up. Elizabeth held in a chuckle as she watched him toddle over. He kind of looked like a frog the way he walked, slightly bobbing up and down and side to side.

"The joust. I will contribute jewels and gold to the purse. The winner takes the girl, horses, jewels, and gold. All."

"I will match your stake."

There was an area roped off. Rabbie told her it was the lists, where the men usually practiced swords.

"Thomas is teaching me to fight." He stood up straight then blushed. She looked to see why, and noticed Joan hurrying across the courtyard.

"Like that, is it?"

The boy looked at her. "Mistress?"

She pointed. "You like Joan."

"Aye, but she says I am much too young for her."

Elizabeth touched his arm. "How old is Joan?"

"She is eleven." He watched the cute girl all way into the hall before turning back to Elizabeth. "I am only ten."

"One year isn't anything much. My mom is twelve years older than my dad. Give her time; she'll come around."

The smile on Rabbie's face made her grin. "I will. Joan is the only woman in all the lands for me."

"You're young. You could meet lots of other pretty girls," she teased him.

"Never. There is only Joan." He looked so certain that it made her momentarily jealous, wishing someone would be as certain of her. To distract herself, Elizabeth pointed to the men below. "Do they do this a lot?"

The boy considered her question. "My lord is very good at the joust. And sword fighting. He is one of the best in England. Has won a great deal of gold. Have no fear; he will win."

A door opened and one of the servants came out bearing a tray. "Lord Highworth bid me bring you spiced wine. He didn't want you to catch a chill."

How unexpected. So he could be kind when he wished. Elizabeth accepted the cup, feeling the warmth seep into her hands. She looked down to find Robert looking up at her. Lifting the cup, she mouthed *thank you* before turning to the servant. "Thanks. It's exactly what I needed."

While she'd been busy thinking about the timeline of history, Robert and Radford had dressed in chainmail, with several plates of armor covering the vulnerable parts of the body. They sat on huge horses, waiting as men brought out long wooden lances.

She could feel the excitement in the air as Rabbie and the guard both leaned forward, watching.

"Come on, beat the whoreson." The guard pounded the gray stone wall with a gloved fist.

She caught some of the crude remarks bantered back and forth as both riders prepared. One of the men called out and they were off. Galloping toward each other, lances down; the earth trembled as the horses thundered onward. The anticipation was infectious, and she leaned forward, clenching the cup in her hands, anxious to see who would win. And what her fate would be. For she had no rights. Was at the mercy of a jerk or a frog. Which was the least worst choice?

Chapter Nineteen

The scene unfolding in front of her made Elizabeth feel like she was standing on a movie set or attending one of those medieval dinners. She'd never been to a Renaissance faire, but imagined it must look similar.

As the horses brought the men closer and closer, Robert teetered back and forth in the saddle.

She squinted. "Is he drunk?"

The guard frowned, but it was Rabbie who spoke up. "No more than usual, mistress."

As if that was supposed to make her feel better. When the frog's lance struck Robert, she couldn't help it: Elizabeth screamed. In slow motion, she watched as he leaned far to the right like a metronome but did not fall, instead coming back to center, leaning to the left, and then returning to an upright position in the saddle.

The pounding of her heart made it hard to hear what the men below were saying. She clenched the cup so tightly she was surprised it didn't shatter into a thousand pieces.

They went again, and she swore her nerves couldn't take it. This time Robert hit Radford, who listed precariously to the side but did not fall. The whole thing was nerve-racking.

Rabbie rubbed his hands together. "'Tis the last time. My lord will take him down now."

Radford's lance struck Robert in the chest so hard he went flying backward off the horse, landing in the mud with a splat. The cloak trimmed in white fur and beautiful embroidery was now covered with muck. At least the mail and armor would wash off.

The inventive swearing made her grin. When Elizabeth made it home she'd have to remember some of them. As she watched, Radford dismounted and bobbled over to Robert, leaning over him. The man had his back to her, so she couldn't see the look on his face or hear what he said. But she knew it had to be bad from the way Robert stiffened.

Then the frog straightened up and, even with his vertically challenged self, managed to look down his nose at everyone. Radford puffed out his chest. "You lose, Thornton. I will have a fine time with my spirited filly. Where is the faerie?"

That horrible little man was talking about her. This

was not good. She couldn't go with him; there was something about him that set off all the warning bells in her head. Elizabeth would have bet her camper and Lulabell that he wasn't a nice guy at all. Some of the richest men were the worst, thinking the law didn't apply to them. That they could do whatever they wished, with no thought to the consequences. Every fiber of her being told her Radford was one of the bad guys.

While Robert had acted like a complete jerk since the night she'd woken up in his bed, at least she knew he wouldn't harm her. Well, other than throwing her in the dungeon, but she guessed it was better than being burnt at the stake for being a witch or a faerie. In this day and age, men thought women of knowledge were evil, so she'd count herself lucky. At least so far.

When Robert made it to his feet, he swayed for a moment. He was a lord with scads of money and a fairytale castle, yet all he wanted to do was laze about, drinking and fooling around. What a waste. Elizabeth thought of everything he could do to make people's lives better. Rabbie had told her a little of the Thornton brothers. It didn't sound like the rest of them behaved like frat boys.

What was up with Robert? There was something bothering him. She knew it like she knew when a coal company was hiding damning information. A gift, her mom said. The ability to see the truth.

The guard turned to her. "I am truly sorry. 'Tis time,

mistress."

There was no other way. She couldn't escape; there were too many men milling around. They would catch her in a second. The dress and cloak slowed her down. She knew. Last night in her chamber she'd run across the room fully dressed, counting the seconds. Then after Joan helped her undress and left, she tried again. So much faster. The voluminous dress and cloak nearly tripped her.

And if she did escape the castle, where would she go? It wasn't like there was a road or car for her to flag down help. There wasn't a way to call for help, either. No phones. *Face it. You're all alone in medieval England without a cent to your name. And the only man you know just doomed you to leave with a disgusting frog.*

As they made their way to the lists, Robert looked sheepish.

"I am sorry, Elizabeth."

She backed away from him. "You're not sorry. If you were, you wouldn't have offered me up as the prize in your stupid little game in the first place."

Lord Radford pranced over. As he opened his mouth to speak, Featherton appeared, a few hairs out of place, which for him meant there was some kind of major disaster. He was so much like the Featherton from her time that a wave of homesickness washed over her, threatening to pull her under and carry her away.

"Are you unwell?"

She saw the concern in Robert's dark blue eyes. Too little, too late. "I'm fine."

Featherton wrung his hands. "The kitchen maid has taken ill. Fever is spreading through the castle."

Right. And she had a lovely swamp for sale. Neither Featherton would ever wring their hands. Not even if the roof collapsed. She pursed her lips, thinking. Illness was something he would whisper about to Robert, keeping it from the guests. But the steward purposely spoke in a loud voice so everyone could hear. Why? What on earth was going on? Did it have anything to do with the mysterious Scot hidden away?

Lord Radford jumped back, holding a cloth over his nose and mouth.

"Come. We depart." He shrieked at his servant to bring his belongings, and bellowed to another for the carriage and horses to be made ready.

The other men quickly followed suit. Rabbie had told her they were minor nobles, third and fourth sons who traveled from estate to estate like locusts feasting on the fields.

Fever was serious. Part of her wanted to yell out, *You think the fever is bad just wait until the plague hits*. But she couldn't. They wouldn't believe her, and she'd likely find herself frantically blowing out the flames beneath her feet. Dread skittered down her back. When had the plague decimated England?

"Think. When was it?" She racked her brain, and a

snippet floated from one of the file drawers to the floor of her head. "The Hundred Years' War comes next. The plague sweeps across England in...1348." She let out a sigh. Fifteen years from now. What if she was stuck in the past? Trapped in time. There would be a front-row seat with her name on it. There she'd have an up close and personal view as the plague ravaged the country. If it didn't kill everyone around her. Including her.

Elizabeth pushed the thought of plague away. Not acceptable. No way did she want to live through such a terrible time.

"Sorry, Mom, there's no adventure or fun in the plague."

Somehow she'd find a way back. Back to her own time. And running water, electricity, and Wi-Fi. When she got home, she'd find adventure, but without swords and men who thought to send up a warm cup of wine when it was cold outside.

Chaos filled the courtyard. No one was paying any attention to her as the guests tried to depart at the same time. Now was her chance. She picked up her skirts and ran. Made it all the way to the first portcullis before a knight caught her by the arm.

She kicked him in the shin, and when he hopped back, she broke free. Though she didn't get very far before Rotten Robert caught her. For a moment she thought she'd barf when he slung her over his shoulder.

"I lost and you will go with him. Do not make me tie

you up. From the moment you arrived, you have been nothing more than an annoyance. I beseech you, mistress. Do not cause me any more trouble."

"I don't care what year it is—you shouldn't be able to sell another human being. It isn't right. I don't care if this is how things are in the past."

She felt his body tense.

"What do you mean 'the past'?" He spoke quietly, as if he knew how dangerous their conversation was. "Why does the year matter?"

Time to backpedal. "You know, you're very archaic. I've seen more modern castles."

"Nay, lady. Highworth is a marvel of its time."

She snorted into his back. "Maybe if I fell through a rabbit hole."

"Lady?"

"Never mind."

Robert held her to him, almost gently. "I did not sell you; Radford won you fairly." Then he paused before adding, "Circumstances change—do not forget that, Elizabeth."

"Whatever."

Then the moment they shared was gone and he dumped her to the ground at the feet of Radford.

"Get in the carriage, girl."

Elizabeth rolled under the carriage, jumped up, and ran. She didn't get very far before Thomas caught her. Leaning close, he whispered in her ear, "There is more at stake here, lady. Robert is not a wicked man. He is doing what he must to keep all of us safe. Even you."

"I don't care what's going on. He can't send me with that odious man. He's mean. I can tell."

"Trust me, lady. Robert is doing what he thinks will keep you from harm."

She pulled free from his hold and walked back to the carriage. A man with greasy-looking brown hair stood in front of her. "Lord Radford says I am to put you in the carriage."

"I can do it myself."

The man leered at her. He threw her over his shoulder, copping a feel. She kicked and screamed, swearing at them all. What was with everyone treating her like a sack of corn? With a grunt, she landed at the feet of Mr. Frog. She was jolted across the floor as the carriage lurched forward.

No matter what, she would find a way to escape. There had to be one kind person in this awful place. If she did find a willing soul, what would she say? The only thing she was sure of was that Highworth was critical to her getting back to her own time. So let Froggy take her to his home; she'd find her way back to Robert's. And Mr. I Know What's Best For You could stuff it.

She might as well try to make the best of the situation until she could figure out a plan. Find the fun and all that bullshit.

"Isn't your name Paul? It seems silly to call you Lord

Radford."

He sputtered, turning red in the face. "You will not address me so familiarly. I am Lord Radford to you, nothing more." He looked her up and down, sneering. "You are no lady. I am supposed to believe you are a faerie, but you have done no magic. Therefore, I will address you as girl or wench."

Frustration got the better of Elizabeth, and she stuck her tongue out at him.

He narrowed his eyes and didn't laugh, as most men would have. "You will be like a wild horse in my bed, wench. I will enjoy breaking you."

The tone of his voice and the look on his face filled her with fear. She was alone in medieval England with no rights and no one to protect her. This man could do with her as he chose and no one would lift a finger to help her. This was sooo not the adventure or the fun she'd hoped for.

Chapter Twenty

Robert blinked, cursing the light. His mouth was dry and his head ached.

"Wine?" His steward flicked a hand in front of his nose.

A discreet sniff told Robert he did not stink. Featherton smirked.

"Do you have to bellow so, Featherton?"

The man banged around the chamber, muttering. Robert rolled to his side and sat up, reaching for the cup. The tableau from last night played in front off his eyes. The look on Elizabeth's face as she was tossed into the carriage. He was an arse. One thing in particular stood out.

Whatever.

A word he had come to know well. A word only a few

used. Elizabeth's tone was full of disdain when she spat the word at him. He'd wanted desperately to tell her why he was behaving like a dolt, but he could not. Radford needed to believe he had won her fairly. If he suspected a ruse, he would sniff around until he found Connor. The man was the worst sort of gossip.

Four interminable days. Each day the same. He woke to scorn from Featherton, rode, crossed swords in the lists, and drank until he required aid to find his chamber. For four days it had been thus. Everyone was tired of him. He was disgusted with himself.

Robert staggered out to the lists. "Who's first?"

A knight stepped forward as Robert unsheathed his sword. The sound of metal on metal made his teeth ache.

"I am sorry, my lord." The knight shrank back, and Robert looked down to see his sleeve turn crimson.

"'Tis naught but a scratch. I would have lost my head if you weren't treating me like a small child. The fault is mine." He waved the man away. One of the servants bound the scratch on his arm. Deciding to take his foul self elsewhere, Robert paced back and forth on the battlements to calm his mood. Usually it worked, but not for the past several days. Thomas joined him.

"Fight like a witless babe for real and you will die. For four days you have moped around the castle. Go and bring the lady back."

"I cannot jeopardize Connor's safety. No matter how

much I worry for her. Future girls are strong. She will be fine."

"Go and fetch her. Tell her why Connor is here. She has secrets of her own. She will keep ours."

Robert stopped pacing. "When did you become so wise?"

Thomas laughed. "I have always been wise. You don't listen."

Robert clapped him on the back. "You're right. I will fetch her." He took a deep breath of icy air.

Thomas put a hand on his arm. "Take men with you. 'Tis not safe to ride alone through the countryside."

"I find my mood improved. To the lists, so I can grind you into the mud." Robert unsheathed his sword. "I would ask you to remain here and keep an eye on our guest. But if it will ease your womanly fears, I will take three of the men."

And for the rest of the afternoon, Robert worked up a sweat. Made preparations to leave the next morning and fetch his Elizabeth back. Future women had fierce tempers; he might needs duck when he explained why he'd been such an arse.

Elizabeth had been escorted to an opulent chamber. Or as she thought of it, a pretty prison. A bath had been brought in and two girls helped her bathe. After three days in a carriage with a man who believed bathing made one ill, it was heavenly to soak in the hot water, relaxing while one of the girls scrubbed her hair. The soap was scented with lavender, helping her to relax. A third girl crept in, carrying some kind of cloth to dry her off. When Elizabeth stepped out of the tub, she noticed the black eye.

"What happened?"

The girl flinched. "Nothing, lady."

"A black eye isn't *nothing*. Who hit you?"

The other women looked around, fearful of being overheard. One of them leaned close to Elizabeth. "Lord Radford is cruel."

The other girl hung the chemise and dress near the fire to warm. "We fear for you, lady."

The one with the black eye started to cry. Elizabeth went to her, heedless of the towel falling. "Tell me. Tell me what's wrong."

One of the women wrapped Elizabeth in a blanket and the four of them sat by the fire.

"His temper is fierce. I broke his prized statue. I didn't mean to. But he..." The girl clutched her arms, her face pink.

Elizabeth patted her shoulder, pulling the girl close.

"You don't have to go on. Did he force you?"

The girl leaned back and looked up at her, tears running down her face. She nodded. And Elizabeth swore. One of the women put a hand to her mouth. "I've never heard such words from a lady."

Elizabeth scowled. "I am not a lady. I'm just a woman, like the rest of you. No means no. A man should listen."

One of the women blinked at her. "He owns us. He can do as he pleases. No one would help us."

The oldest of the three—she looked about seventeen—said, "Three of the kitchen maids have given birth to his babes. All girls. Which infuriates him all the more."

Elizabeth stood. "Help me dress. I do not wish him to find me like this." She held up the dress. It was gray and trimmed in fur. "He lays a hand on me and he'll lose it."

There had to be a way to help these women. But she didn't know how. Her main thought was escaping, and if she escaped, how could she do them any good? Then again, how could she help them by being locked up in this chamber? She'd have to find a way to escape and get help. To come back and help these women. She didn't care what century it was. No meant no.

And if Lord Radford thought he could have her, he could think again. For it would be a cold day in hell before he laid a froggy finger on her skin.

Chapter Twenty-One

The guards roughly tossed Elizabeth to the floor of the chamber. "Ow. Thanks, guys. I really wanted this knee to match the other."

The door shut, the key turning in the lock. Not a very cheery bunch. Her knee and hip ached, the bruises a lovely purple-blue, but Elizabeth smiled through the throbbing pain. This was the fifth day she'd survived without Radford touching her.

Every night they dined together and then he would make a pass at her. And that was when she got it through her head...she wasn't like the servants. Because if she was, he would've forced her. None of the servants or guards would lift a finger to help if she screamed. They'd go about their business, pretending they didn't hear what the high and mighty lord was doing.

Thank goodness things would change in the years to come. Men still took advantage of women, but at least women had rights. When she made it back home, she'd vote in every election and speak out for women. Her mother had protested when she was younger. Before going to live with her grandmother or on one of her parent's trips back home, Elizabeth remembered helping her mom make signs at the kitchen table. While other kids were playing with dolls and trucks, she was coming up with pithy slogans and watching her mom fight for what she believed in. It was an unconventional upbringing, but it had suited her, and Elizabeth believed her childhood was helping her cope with finding her way in the past.

Her captor was shorter than her by almost five inches, but he had a good eighty to a hundred pounds on her. All he had to do was sit on Elizabeth and she'd be unable to move.

The first night when he slobbered over her, he'd been rewarded with a cup of wine to the face. The second night when he pulled her down on his lap, she'd dumped a bowl of soup on his head. And the third night, she wasn't proud of her actions, but after he'd ripped her dress and gotten grabby, she bit him. Hard enough to draw blood. She'd gotten a split lip in return, but he left her alone. That was what he got for trying to cop a feel.

Last night was the fourth night. And it was the first time she'd felt bone-chilling fear since arriving. The creep had cornered her in an alcove and pinned her there. Standing so close she couldn't get a knee up. So she pretended to give in. Let him kiss her. As he slobbered all over her face and neck, she'd pretended to hold his hand. As if the disgusting man could believe she found him appealing.

Then she took hold of his little finger and bent it back hard enough to hear the crack. He fell to his knees, yelping in pain. For good measure, she kicked him in the gut before taking off running. When she hurdled a kneeling servant scrubbing the floor, her skirts caught and she went down hard. Her elbow hit just right and pain arced through her body. And that was when the guards caught her. Carried her kicking and screaming to the chamber and tossed her to the floor, locking the door. At least she'd gotten one guy in the face and another in the gut on the way. Later, Radford opened the door, surrounded by guards. Smart man. He bellowed, swearing tomorrow night he would have her. The guards would hold her down, and when he was finished, he'd give her to them.

She'd stayed defiant until he left. Then she collapsed, shaking on the bed. There was no way she would end up as a victim. Elizabeth had experienced her fair share of drunken frat boys during college. Learned how to put them in their place when they didn't want to hear no. She was a grown woman and knew where to hit for maximum impact to protect herself. As far as she was concerned, all girls should be required to take self-defense classes in high school.

"Thank you, Mom and Dad." She clasped her hands together, thinking of her parents. They'd insisted her grandmother send her to the class. So she could look out for herself. Elizabeth would be forever grateful. Those classes had likely saved her since she'd landed in the past. Decision made, Elizabeth prowled the room, looking for any potential weapons she might have missed. Tomorrow she was escaping. And she was stealing the serving girls, if they'd come.

The next day after the midday meal, Lord Radford came to her chamber. But not alone. He'd learned his lesson and now showed up with several guards. He was apologetic. Blamed it on the drink. And since she needed to be out of the locked chamber to escape, she widened her eyes. Looked at the floor and then up at him.

"My behavior was most unladylike. Please forgive me, my lord. Might we dine together tonight? The two of us, alone?" She fluttered her eyes at him. He took a step closer, licking his thin lips.

"I will have a feast prepared." He ran a hand down her arm before leaving the room. Once the lock turned, she made a gagging noise. No wonder he wasn't married. He probably drowned any prospective brides in slobber. Elizabeth forced herself to take a nap, knowing she might be running through the woods all night if her plan worked. There was a muddy path leading from the castle toward the woods, and she hoped with an almost full moon tonight, there would be enough light for her to see where she was going.

"Please don't let it snow."

The sound of the door opening made her hop out of bed.

"I'm to dress you for supper." It was only the girl with the black eye.

"Thank you. How's the eye today?"

The girl touched her fingers to her cheekbone. "It no longer hurts, lady. I should not have said anything."

Elizabeth touched the girl's face. When she met her gaze, Elizabeth said, "Somehow I will find a way to help you. We could escape."

"You mustn't. He has a terrible temper."

She patted the girl's arm. "Let me worry about that."

The girl wiped a tear away. "We cannot go with you, lady, but if you get free, we will not tell."

They were too scared. So as much as Elizabeth wanted to take the serving girls with her, she knew she could not. Once she was free, she'd find some way to help them.

When the girl left, Elizabeth spoke to one of the guards. The men escorted her down the stairs to Radford's chamber.

"My lord will be but a moment. Do not touch anything." The guard sneered at her. She was left alone in the overdone room. Elizabeth prowled around the room, looking for anything that might be used as a weapon. But there wasn't much to work with. A bed, a chest at the foot of the bed, a table, and two chairs. The pitcher on the small table by the bed caught her eye. That would do nicely.

In the corner of the room, was a large rectangle covered with a rough-looking brown cloth. It hadn't been there before. Moving closer, she heard what sounded like a soft sob. That was no animal. Elizabeth knelt down in front of the cage and lifted the cloth. Big brown eyes blinked back at her. She yanked the cloth off and covered her mouth.

"Oh my goodness. What are you doing in there?"

Chapter Twenty-Two

The cage held a small boy who couldn't have been more than six or seven. He wiped his eyes and looked at her. "Are you going to eat me, lady?"

Elizabeth couldn't help it. She burst out laughing. "Eat you? Don't be silly. I'm not a wicked witch with a house made of candy."

The boy blinked at her. "A house made of candy? I've never heard such a thing. You're a faerie." He pointed to her hair. "Don't take me under the faerie hill. I don't want to spend the rest of my days under the ground."

She laughed again. Laughed for the first time in days, so hard her stomach ached. "I am not a witch and I am not a faerie. Now tell me, what is your name and why are you in a cage?"

The boy sat hunched over, unable to sit up straight.

"My name is Gavin, my lady."

"I am Elizabeth. Now tell me why you are here and I will do what I can to help you."

The boy was wearing some kind of long tunic and loose-fitting pants made out of coarse tan cloth. His shoes looked worn, but she didn't see any holes in them. He needed a haircut and had dirt on his face. He looked like a little street urchin who'd stepped out of the pages of a book.

"I'm from London. My mam died of the fever. Men came and took our things, turned me out in the streets, so I lived behind the abattoir. When the man found me, he threw me into the street. But I wasn't sad; it smelled terrible back there and I stank of death."

"I'm sorry about your mom. How did you meet Lord Radford?"

The boy wiped his nose on his sleeve. "I was living on the streets, making my living as a pickpocket. I took my lord's pouch and would've gotten away, but I tripped over a pile of dung."

She grinned at him. "It doesn't sound like you're a very good pickpocket."

He scowled at her. "Nay, lady. I am the best pickpocket in all of London. The only reason I did not escape was because I fell into the shit. It was a pile this tall." He stretched his hands from the floor to the top of the cage.

She laughed again, clapping a hand over her mouth

and biting down on her cheek to hold the giggle in when she heard voices at the door. With a finger to her lips, she whispered, "Quiet. I will find a way to free you."

The boy leaned close to the bars. "He keeps the key on a ring he wears round his waist."

Elizabeth nodded as she straightened the cloth. Hurrying over to the fire, she stood there as if she didn't have a care in the world. Servants bustled into the room, bearing food. Her stomach growled.

"Smells delicious." She forced a smile to her face as he pulled her close, snuffling her hair. Catching a whiff of Radford, she barely refrained from gagging. The odor of rotten meat and body odor permeated the air.

"I see you have come to your senses. Would you care for a drink?"

"Yes, please. What is under the cloth?"

He didn't even look over. "A curiosity I picked up on my travels to London. Nothing to concern yourself with."

As they ate, Elizabeth kept glancing at the cage. She made sure to leave enough on her plate for the child.

The boy sneezed, and it was the opening she needed. "Is there a person in there? What terrible crime did they commit?"

Radford sneered. "'Tis nothing but a common thief. I have not yet decided what to do with him."

"We should feed him. I'm sure he must be hungry."

Lord Radford tried to look apologetic and failed

miserably. “I have eaten all. There is none to share.”

She reached across the table, taking his clammy, sweaty hand in hers. “Would you mind terribly if I gave him the rest of my meal? I cannot eat it all, and your food is so wonderful. I would hate to waste what’s left.”

She leaned forward, giving him a good view of her cleavage. “Surely one as great as you would show a small kindness to such a wretched creature.”

He licked his lips, his eyes never moving from her neckline.

“If it pleases you, feed the child.”

She took the plate over, lifted the cloth, and set the dish down outside the bars.

“Thank you, my lord. My lady.” The boy reached through the bars, snatching pieces of bread, stuffing meat and vegetables into his mouth as fast as he could. She wondered when he’d last eaten. Once he finished, she took the plate, winked at him, pulled the cloth back over the bars, and placed the plate on the table. Froggy had poured her another glass of wine. There was a soft knock and two servants came to clear the remains of the meal.

“Leave the wine.” He waved a hand. “Do not disturb us. No matter what you hear.”

The guard leaned into the chamber. “Shall I stay, my lord?”

Lord Radford smiled the same grin Elizabeth imagined the wolf did before he gobbled up the grandmother. “Nay. Seek your bed. I will have no further need of you tonight. The lady will please me this eve.”

Disgusting. She sat back in the chair, asking him questions about himself. He talked and talked, boasting of his many estates and how wealthy he was before finally setting his cup down. He faked the worst yawn she’d ever seen as he stretched.

“I find I am most tired.”

She wanted to throw up, but smiled brightly. Let him lead her to the bed.

“Let me.” She unbuttoned his jacket. The garment was so tight it left red marks on his big white belly. He was so busy drooling over her chest that he wasn’t paying attention to her hands. She reached over, picked up the ceramic pitcher, and conked him on the head.

He crumpled to the floor. No one entered, so she knelt down, unhooking the ring of keys from the jeweled belt at his waist. After a moment’s hesitation, she took the pouch too. It was heavy, the coins inside clinking together. She’d need the money to pay for lodging on her journey. On the third try, the lock clicked, the door swung open, and the boy tumbled out of the nasty cage.

His eyes were huge. “Did you kill ’im?”

“No. But he’s going to have a terrible headache when he wakes. Now be quiet and follow me. We’re getting out of here.”

She went to the door and cracked it open. There was

no one in the hall. "Stay behind me and be quiet." In the hall, men slept close to the hearths. Keeping to the wall, she and Gavin made their way to the kitchens.

The cloth from her hair would serve as a makeshift bag. Bread, cheese, and what else? As she looked around, the boy popped out of an alcove. He had a jug tucked under each arm. A young girl slept curled up by the fire.

Elizabeth had also stolen both of Lord Radford's cloaks for she and the boy. There was a door in the kitchen, but she hesitated.

The boy tugged at her dress. "It will lead us outside, lady. This is where they brought me in."

The door opened without a squeak, the cold night air making her gasp. Creeping along the wall, they stayed in shadow. From what she could see, there were only two men on duty on top of the gate.

"Look, lady. The portcullis was not closed all the way this night."

A shape against the wall moved, and she made out a man wrapped in his cloak. He hunched over a small fire set in some kind of metal basket. As they moved closer, she saw his head resting on his chest, heard the soft snores. She tiptoed past him. The boy grinned, dropped to the ground, and rolled under the gate, never dropping either jug and looking like an overgrown ghost wrapped up in the voluminous cloak.

Crossing her fingers she would fit, Elizabeth did the

same. The cold metal of the pointed spikes dragged against the cloak as she scooted through the opening.

Her heart was beating so loudly she was sure the guards would hear. The boy moved and she grabbed his arm, pointed up. "Wait until they turn the other way, then we run for the trees."

One man went left and the other right, making their rounds. Elizabeth tugged on Gavin's arm and they ran. No shouts rang out after them. The gate remained as it was, so she assumed they had not been seen. Leaning over, hands on her knees, wheezing, Elizabeth gasped for breath.

Now all they had to do was figure out where to go. The only place she knew was Highworth, and she truly believed it held the key to her return to her own time. What was the saying? The devil you know is better than the one you don't?

"Where to? London?"

Elizabeth hoped she was making the right choice. "No. We're going to Highworth Castle. They will take us in."

What she didn't tell him was that she wasn't sure what kind of reception they would receive. But at this point she didn't care. She would force Robert to let them stay until she figured out where to go. And if he didn't want to listen? There was a heavy pitcher in her chamber. She'd knock him over the head too. Tie him up and threaten him until he helped her, took in Gavin, and rescued the three serving girls from Radford.

Chapter Twenty-Three

Up ahead, three ruffians stood around a bundle on the ground as Robert's instincts told him not to tarry. He urged the beast forward, the horses trampling the newly fallen snow. Robert jumped to the ground, tossing the reins to one of the men.

"Stay with the horses. You two, with me."

A man dressed in rags, with a long, matted beard and several missing teeth, charged him. He wore a tattered belt and jerked at the sword, trying to free it from the scabbard.

"The cold," Robert rasped. "Sometimes it makes the blade stick." He unsheathed his blade, running the man through. The other two were dispatched quickly, their blood staining the snow, eyes open and unseeing. A fourth man dropped from a nearby tree and ran, but he was no match for Robert's knight, who took aim and let the arrow fly. The ruffian went down, falling into the snow without a sound.

A brilliant lock of blue hair, bright against the snow, made Robert's heart wrench inside his chest. He stumbled forward, falling to his knees, beseeching the fates. His stomach full of eels, he gritted his teeth. "Elizabeth. Can you hear me?"

Saints, let her be unharmed. He needed her at Highworth. Robert lifted her, saw her arms clutched protectively around another bundle. One that squirmed and moved. Her eyes flickered, then opened.

"Oh, it's you. I'm mad at you, you big jerk."

He chuckled. "You've every right to be. I will explain everything, but first we must get you warm."

The boy looked like he'd been dragged through the street. "Who have we here?"

He did not let the worry show on his face. But she was so pale, her lips almost as white as her skin.

"That's Gavin." She sighed and closed her eyes, mumbling. "I'm so very tired."

Robert shook her. "Nay. Elizabeth, you must stay awake."

She'd been protecting a child, no doubt from Radford. Robert had much to atone for.

The boy rubbed his eyes. "She saved me from his lordship. Me name's Gavin." He leaned toward Robert. "I'm a pickpocket. From London. Best around."

Of course he was. “Good to know. If ever I have need of your services, I will remember.” Robert had to ask: “Did Radford let you go?”

“You should’ve seen her, my lord. She bashed him over the head. I thought for sure she killed him dead.”

“In truth?”

“I didn’t kill him, but I wish I had.” She wrapped her hand in his. The cold of her touch seeped through his body. He must not tarry.

“Gavin comes with us. Promise me you’ll save them,” she murmured as she fell back asleep.

He shook her again. “Elizabeth. Wake.” But she did not, and worry churned through him. Taking her in his arms, he spoke to one of the men. “Take the boy.”

He settled her on the horse in front of him, wrapping his cloak around them both. “’Tis not far. We passed an inn on our way to bring you home.”

She did not wake. It took them longer than he would’ve liked to make their way to the inn. Knowing she’d escaped Radford, that the man would be after her, Robert bellowed at the innkeeper for rooms. He sent one of the men to see to the horses, and when he told Gavin to go to the stables, the boy pulled a small knife from somewhere on his person.

“I stay with the lady. She saved me, so I owe her my life.”

Robert could appreciate the debt. “Then you shall be her personal guard. Do not let any harm come to our lady."

The boy stood up straight, raising his chin. "You can rely on me." He scampered up the stairs, unharmed from the ordeal and snow, as Elizabeth had used her body to shield the lad from the cold.

In the small room, a woman knelt, stoking the fire. "My wife requires a bath. She was out in the snow. We must warm her."

The woman dusted her hands on her dress. "I shall see to it. I'll bring food and drink for ye, my lord."

"Gavin. Tell the men we leave in the morning. There is a storm coming, and I want to be home before it hits."

Robert didn't know what made him do it. To say she was his wife. Nay, that wasn't true. He'd said it because of her reputation. He did not want the innkeeper and the servants to think she was a woman without virtue. 'Twas the first step to making all right with her.

Robert settled Elizabeth on his lap in front of the fire. He rubbed her hands, removed her boots, and rubbed her frozen feet, noticing the pink paint coming off her toes. Once he had heard Anna and Charlotte talking, and they said 'twas called polish. The normally pale skin of his lady was even whiter. He marveled at the unblemished and unmarked skin, smooth as a babe.

At last she stirred. "Where are we?" She blinked up at him.

"We cannot travel in the dark. I have acquired rooms at an inn. Don't worry; we'll be safe here, and in the morning we will resume our travels."

"But he'll find us."

Robert shook his head. "Nay. I sent a messenger to Radford. The man will say you were seen traveling north, towards Leeds. And we go south to Highworth." He brushed a lock of purple hair behind her ear. "What were you thinking? You could have frozen to death, been assaulted or killed. Your death would have been a tragedy of immense proportions."

"So now you're concerned for my welfare? Why now? You've been nothing but an ass since I woke up in your bed." She shifted and he pulled her closer, holding her until she stilled.

"I should not have let you go." He held himself stiffly, knowing he was wrong.

She sighed. "I should hate you for how you've treated me, but I find my need for answers outweighs my anger."

He touched a finger to her cheek, pleased to see the color slowly returning to her beautiful face. "In time, Elizabeth. I swear, in time."

The scent of roses filled the air as the serving girls filled the bathing tub with steaming water.

"Shall we help you into the bath, lady?"

Robert answered, "Nay, I will see to my wife."

The door shut and she scowled at him. "Wife?"

"I did not want your virtue questioned. Can you stand? Your bath is ready."

She groaned, teeth chattering. He looked to her hair as his lips twitched and he coughed.

"What's so funny?"

He couldn't help it: he threw back his head and laughed. "'Tis your hair. It matches your lips."

"It isn't funny." She sniffed. But he saw the twitch of her mouth as she tried to hold the laughter at bay.

Elizabeth touched the sleeves of her dress. "I can't undress by myself."

The thought of her bare skin made him swallow hard. Was it as soft and unblemished all over? "I will call the girl back to help you."

As she swayed on her feet, he caught her in his arms. Green eyes looked into his, into the depths of his soul and his black heart. Did she see the ugly truth of him?

"No. You'll have to help me. I'm about to fall asleep again."

He didn't want to admit how worried he was about her, so he nodded. "I will do my best not to look upon your form, lady."

"I care not. Where I come from, being nude is no big deal." At the look on his face, she touched a finger to the corner of his mouth. "After all, we all have a body. A face and lips. All men are basically the same, and so are all women." He watched her mouth twitch, heard the giggle escape.

"The lady is amused?"

Elizabeth chewed her lip. "Froggy. Now, he is not like

you at all. His belly is like Jell-O and he smells, but you, you have the most amazing stomach. I could run my fingers across your abs for days."

Robert didn't know what Jell-O was, but understood it wasn't complimentary. "You find my form pleasing?"

As she swayed back and forth, she pretended to gag. "Wouldn't you like to know? Now get me into the bath. I feel like an ice cube."

He helped her undress, swallowing as his fingers encountered bare skin. She was still cool to the touch, but he no longer worried like a woman. Robert thanked the fates for not letting her die, for him finding her in the snow.

As he undid the last button and helped her out of the dress, she stood in front of the fire in nothing but her chemise. The fire and candlelight turned the garment transparent, showing him every curve. His mouth went dry. She was so beautiful. Seeing her so close to death unlocked something within him. He didn't want to admit he cared for her, but he knew it was thus. Mayhap the moment he woke next to her, she had stolen his heart.

He turned his back as she slipped out of the chemise. Imagining what she must look like, he thought of all manner of unpleasant things to distract him.

"Do you require assistance into the bath?" He heard a splash followed by a groan and turned to see her in the tub, up to her chin.

Robert handed her a cloth with which to wash, and a small ball of soap. She took it and sniffed. “I thought I smelled roses.”

“I brought it with me remembering how much you like to bathe. Roses remind me of you.”

“They do? Why?”

“While they are beautiful, they have thorns and will draw blood if you reach out and take without being careful.” He pressed his lips together. “I am filled with regret for my treatment of you, my lady.”

A servant knocked on the door and entered laden down with trays of food. “Do you need anything else, my lord?”

“No. Thank you for all you have done.” Before Robert could close the door, Gavin slipped inside, looking around.

“Where is my lady?”

Robert pointed. “Your lady is having a bath. Are you hungry?”

Elizabeth snickered. “He’s a boy. He’s always hungry.”

“Take a plate to your lady and then you may eat.”

Gavin piled a plate high and brought it over to her. “I’ll fetch you a cup of wine.”

When he came back and sat down, Robert poured the boy a cup of ale.

“Tell me about yourself. How you came to be with Lord Radford. How you and the lady escaped.”

Between mouthfuls of food, the boy told his tale. When he finished, Robert sat back, elbows on the rough table, fingers under his chin. Gavin took the empty plate from Elizabeth and refilled the wooden cup. "You're going to be all wrinkled. Don't you want to get out?"

Robert couldn't stop looking at her. The color was back in her cheeks, her lips no longer blue. She looked like a water goddess come to life.

"I'm getting out now."

The boy looked horrified. "We must leave the room, lady. 'Tis not proper."

Robert chuckled. "The lady has peculiar ideas about what is proper and what is not. Turn your back, but hand her a drying cloth when she gets out."

Gavin made a face but did as he was told. Robert peeked out of the corner of his eye. He couldn't resist. She was well formed and shapely. How he ached to kiss her again, had thought of her lips on his ever since she woke in his bed. He swallowed. There would be hell to pay for her escaping Radford. But 'twas his fault, and he would see it made right.

"Hand me the chemise, will you?"

Robert stopped the boy. "She will not wear anything from Radford. I brought her clothes to wear. In the satchel on the bed."

Gavin rummaged through the sack, pulling out clothes. "Shall I fetch a girl to help you dress, lady?"

"I can manage, but I'll need you to do up the buttons.

Think you can handle that?"

The boy stood up straight. "Aye, lady. My lord says I am to guard you, so I will be here for you always."

Once Elizabeth was dressed, she sat down in a chair in front of the fire, the tiredness evident in her face.

"Go and seek your bed in the stables, Gavin."

The boy shook his head. "Nay. I will not leave the lady to sleep in the room with you alone, my lord."

He caught Elizabeth's eye. She winked.

"You can sleep in front of the fire."

Robert ran a hand through his hair, tired from riding hard the past three days. "You should not have run. I was coming for you." He looked at the boy. "Nor should you. You are Lord Radford's property."

He looked back in time to see Elizabeth's eyes flash. "Human beings are not property." She took another drink and set the cup down with a bang. "I know here in your time they are, but where I come from people are free. It is difficult for me to see people treated badly. There are three girls I left behind. We have to help them."

Robert had a bad feeling as Elizabeth went on to explain to him why he had to rescue the girls. Horror filled him. He knew of many lords who dallied with the serving girls. Many illegitimate babes born of such encounters. But the way she described how he forced himself on the servants, beat them, made Robert's stomach turn. He was a dolt.

"You have strange notions, Elizabeth. Don't you think it's time to tell me where you are from? How you came to be at Highworth, in my bed?" He looked down, but Gavin was fast asleep in front of the fire.

She yawned. "Tomorrow. I'll tell you tomorrow. Let me sleep."

He carried her to the bed and covered her up. "Never fear, lady. I will find a place to sleep with the men."

She grabbed his sleeve. "Please. Don't leave us alone."

Robert knew he should not stay, but the look in her eyes made him reconsider.

She patted the bed. "It's big enough for both of us. You stay on your side and I will stay on mine. We are both dressed. There is nothing wrong with you sleeping next to me."

The thought of sleeping close to her, those luscious curves only a hairsbreadth away, made Robert swear. He yanked a blanket from the bed. "Nay, I will sleep next to Gavin, in front of the fire."

She shrugged, and he didn't know if it was hurt he saw in her eyes or something else. "As you wish."

As Robert made his bed in front of the fire, he kept stealing glances at Elizabeth. Part of him wanted nothing more than to take her home and keep her safe.

Forever. But the other part of him warned him: *Get rid of her. She will be in danger at Highworth. Connor is not well enough to travel yet.* As Robert fell asleep, he wondered what to do about the meddlesome lady who had captured his heart and soul.

Chapter Twenty-Four

When Elizabeth woke, the first thing that ran through her thoughts was she was finally warm again. She and Gavin had made good time as they'd escaped from Radford's clutches. Instead of spending any of the stolen gold, they'd spent the first night in an abandoned cottage. It was the second day when she'd grown careless.

All the walking in the cold made her sleepy. Gavin had twisted his ankle when he tripped over a half-buried tree limb and was limping, making the going even slower. Used to being outside in harsh conditions during protests, she thought she was in good shape. But this was not walking; this was hiking over hills and through mud and snow. She was exhausted.

When they came upon a small stand of trees, they

agreed to stop for the night. Anything to get out of the biting wind. The brush not only helped with the wind, it sheltered them from anyone out and about. They'd encountered a few travelers but hurried past each other, eager to get to their respective destinations. In case Radford's men were close, they didn't dare build a fire. Gavin huddled next to her, the cold sending them to sleep. She should've known better than to go to sleep in the ice and snow.

On the third day, she'd been awakened by pain shooting up her side. A pile of rags was kicking her. The smell of unwashed bodies made her gag, and by the time she was coherent, they were surrounded.

The men were dressed in little more than tatters, with matted beards full of twigs and things she didn't want to think about. Before she could stop herself, Elizabeth screamed, imagining they were characters out of *Game of Thrones*, come to kill her. The leader was difficult to understand, and she kept getting distracted by the number of teeth he was missing. All of them were missing several if not most of their teeth. One of the four shimmied up a tree as lookout. The leader with the black beard wore an old-looking sword in a scabbard at his waist.

The other two looked at her, the lust clear on their faces. Not only had she worried for her own safety, but also for Gavin's. The men were discussing what to do with them when *he* arrived. Elizabeth had never been so glad to see the odious man.

By then her hands and feet had gone numb. She vaguely remembered Robert drawing his sword. The man falling. When she'd come back to herself, she was in a rose-scented bath, with vague memories of drooling over Robert's abs. The bed linens weren't the cleanest, not to mention kind of scratchy, but to her it was a five-star room. The warmth from the roaring fire was bliss. When she woke again, Robert and Gavin had gone, leaving a serving girl waiting quietly.

"I'm to help ye dress, lady."

The girl was efficient, and while she did up the buttons, Elizabeth's stomach growled.

"You can break your fast below—unless you wish me to bring you a tray?"

"Lead the way."

In the short time she'd been here, she'd come to enjoy drinking warm spiced wine for breakfast. There was a hearty bowl of porridge, and she decided whenever she made it back to her own time, she would eat the stuff in the winter. It stuck to her ribs, keeping her full until lunch. No, dinner, she corrected herself. Dinner or supper. To her those words meant the evening meal, but here dinner was lunch.

On the way outside to look for Robert, she caught sight of the innkeeper's wife in a back room, putting some kind of black goo on her hair.

"I'm sorry to intrude. Are you coloring your hair?"

The woman wiped a spot of black off her cheek. "Aye, I darken it to hide the gray. I know it's vain, but I was quite a beauty when I was young and I don't like growing old."

"My grandmother used to say it's hell getting old." Elizabeth stepped further into the small room. "Could you help me?" She reached up and pulled the cloth off her hair.

The woman gasped and crossed herself. "Is it true, then? Are ye a faerie?"

Used to the reaction, Elizabeth touched her hair, anxious to be rid of the head-turning colors. "No, I'm like you. I wanted a change, and this is what happened after too many drinks late one night."

"A man, was it?"

Elizabeth nodded.

"We best change it back, then."

"Growing up, my hair was brown." Elizabeth sniffed at the mixture in the bowl. "What's in it? Is it permanent?"

The woman had a stained cloth wrapped around her neck to keep the dye off her dress. She gestured to Elizabeth to sit on a nearby stool.

"A bit of this and that. Plants, bark, minerals, and walnuts."

"It smells medicinal. Like something I used to use at home." It reminded her of a shampoo she liked. As much as she'd had fun with the rainbow-colored hair, it was a distraction and a problem here in the past. Everyone assumed she was a faerie or a witch, either of which could get her burnt at the stake. And people tended to avoid her.

The woman rummaged around in a box, came up with another cloth, and draped it around Elizabeth's shoulders and neck. "To keep the mixture off your beautiful dress."

"How long will it take?"

"An hour or so. I'll send my girl to tell your husband you'll be a while."

Elizabeth refrained from correcting her, remembering he had checked them in as husband and wife. For a man who said he despised her, he'd gone out of his way to help her. If he hated her so much, why did he come after her? Why save her?

If he was as nice to her as he was to his servants and men, she knew she'd be head over heels. It was only her he treated so rotten. Did she remind him of an ex?

Elizabeth remembered her first job. She was a senior in high school and her grandmother helped her land a job working for a big law firm. During the first week, one of the female partners had taken an instant dislike to her. A week later Elizabeth found out it was because she looked just like the woman's nanny. And the husband had been cheating with the nanny. Left his wife for the girl half his age. When Elizabeth found out, she resigned, understanding why the woman reacted the way she did. There was no way she wanted to be miserable at work, not when she'd be spending a huge portion of her day there.

Her parents had been horrified when she interned at the law firm, so they were thrilled when she quit. They didn't care why. When she landed the nonprofit gig, they were ecstatic. Proud as could be when she was arrested the first time for protesting contaminated water.

The woman checked on Elizabeth's hair. The mixture was surprisingly warm and a bit tingly on her scalp.

"I brought ye some ale. Your husband knows you're getting ready."

"But won't he wonder what's taking so long?"

The woman eyed her. "You haven't been married long, have ye? Women take their time and men wait. 'Tis the way of the world."

Elizabeth laughed, and they clinked cups. Knowing Robert would have to wait as the mixture did its job, she propped an elbow on the table and relaxed, pondering the mystery of the Scot and the man with dark blue eyes who made her want to scream and smile at the same time.

"I'll be back in a bit to wash it all out, and then we'll have you right as rain."

"Your color is so pretty. No one would ever know you had any gray."

The woman touched a hand to her wet hair. "Thank

ye. The dye will last until your hair grows out." She squinted at Elizabeth's head. "Don't suppose any more colors will show up?"

"Nope." She grinned at the woman.

Gavin skidded to a stop, gaping. "Wot are ye doin', lady?" He leaned over her, sniffing. "Stinks."

"I rather like the smell. Thought it was time for a change." She pointed to the innkeeper's wife out in the main room. "She was kind enough to make my hair brown again."

He looked disappointed. "Guess you're not a witch."

"Nope."

Gavin looked hopeful. "A faerie, then?"

Elizabeth winked at him. "Afraid not. Just a plain, normal girl."

He stood there, rocking back on his heels, hands on his hips, and she suppressed a laugh. Talk about a serious case of hero worship. He'd obviously been studying Robert. Gavin looked just like the man when he was thinking about something or trying not to shout at her, especially as he stroked his chin.

"My lady, there is nothing plain about you."

He was going to be a total heartbreaker when he grew up. She wanted to pull him close and hug him, but was afraid of getting dye on him, so instead she touched Gavin's cheek. "It's a lovely compliment. Thank you."

He cocked an ear toward the door. "I hear the horses. I will go and see if my lord is ready to depart." He turned back and looked at her. “When do you wash it out?”

The innkeeper bustled in. “Right now, laddie. Tell your lord his lady wife will be out soon.”

Chapter Twenty-Five

Robert had sent Gavin to check on Elizabeth while the men readied the horses. He'd gone upstairs to make sure she hadn't forgotten anything in the room. As soon as they returned to Highworth, he would gift her with a new cloak, for he hated seeing her wearing Radford's. Featherton had offered to pack for Elizabeth, but Robert wanted to do it himself. Like a dolt, he thought to bring clothing, but no cloak. Busy making sure she had not left a hair ribbon behind, he knelt down to pick up one of the buttons from her dress. A sound made him reach for his sword, but 'twas not in time, as pain lanced through him and everything went dark.

Rough timbers came into view as Robert blinked. Reaching up to touch his aching head, his fingers came away red. With a grunt, he sat up, the pouch at his waist missing. No wonder his head pained him so. The pitcher was shattered on the floor next to him. Who had hit him over the head and why? Elizabeth.

He bolted to his feet, stumbled, and raced down the stairs, bellowing for his men. "Where is Elizabeth?"

As he ran into the courtyard, three men rode away. "Whoresons." As much as he wanted to go after them, he could not afford to send his men, nor tarry any longer. Radford would have men after them, and they needed to get back to Highworth before the storm hit. He did not want to travel in snow and muck.

When he didn't think life could get any worse, he checked the saddlebags of his horse. The bag of gold was missing.

"What were you dolts doing? I have been robbed."

One of the men looked sheepish. "He said he was feeding the animals, my lord. We did not know he had stolen your gold."

Another man shrugged. "Who leaves gold in the stables?"

And, of course, none of the men had any gold with them to pay the bill.

Elizabeth ran out, her hair wet. "What's wrong? I heard you yelling."

Gavin danced around her, embellishing the tale. "The bandits could have killed my lord. They smashed the pitcher down on his head. He is lucky his head was not smashed open like a melon. And they've stolen all his gold. He can't pay the bill."

"Off with their heads," she shouted, then caught his startled look. "Sorry, I've been dying to say that since I arrived. How do you not abuse the power? I'd be terribly tempted."

A smile tugged at the corner of his face.

"'Tis a great burden to bear." Robert was only half teasing.

She raised a brow at him. "So we have no money? Are we to stay and work off the charges?"

Robert frowned. "I will speak to the innkeeper. When he hears I am Lord Highworth, my word will be enough."

"I'm sure they need the money." Elizabeth rummaged around in her cloak and came up with a pouch. "This ought to do it." She tossed the pouch to him. He caught it with one hand. It was heavy, and when Robert opened it, he saw the gold.

"How?"

She grinned. "I stole it from Froggy."

Robert blew out his cheeks and opened his eyes wide as he made a croaking noise in the back of his throat. Her mouth twitched. She put a hand up to her lips, then turned away, shaking. Snorts of laughter escaped. He joined in.

"Oh my gosh, you looked just like him when you made that face."

"I will settle our account and we will be off. It smells

like snow."

One of the men spoke up. "I told him a storm is coming, lady. My shoulder always aches when a storm approaches."

Robert explained to her, "He was wounded in battle several years ago, and since then we always know when bad weather is coming. His shoulder is never wrong."

He paid the innkeeper and his wife, adding a few extra coins for their trouble and the damage. In the courtyard, Elizabeth was settled on her own horse, Gavin in front of her.

"You are able to ride?"

"A friend of mine has a farm with many horses. I learned years ago. Are we ready to go?"

He held the pouch up for her.

"No, you keep it. We might need it on the way. I only took it in case I needed to secure lodging for Gavin and I as we made our way back to Highworth."

He turned in the saddle. "You were coming back?"

"You didn't want me to?"

"I did—" The wind blew the hood of her cloak back and he blinked. "Your hair. I thought it looked darker. What have you done?"

She touched the dark strands. "You don't like it?"

He spoke without thinking. "It's a rather solid brown. Like the earth in the garden." Robert stared at her face. "Your nose is overlong and your teeth are big for your mouth. With your hair, you remind me of my favorite horse."

Fury turned her emerald eyes the color of a stormy sea. Too late, he realized his error. What was it about her? With all the women before, he paid them compliments, and they swooned. But Elizabeth? Robert opened his mouth and spoke utter nonsense. He was witless around her. In truth, he hadn't meant to insult her; he loved his horse and he liked her nose and teeth.

The color rose up in her cheeks as she fisted her cloak, yet all he could think of was hauling her off the horse and into his arms, kissing her senseless, begging her pardon. But that would be ridiculous, wouldn't it?

"I am not a horse. I don't understand why you're nice to everyone else and so mean to me." She turned away from him.

"Horses are valuable. 'Twas a compliment."

"I give you gold to pay our bill and this is how you treat me." She sneered at him. "I have heard all about the women you bed. How you are the most charming of all the Thornton brothers. Yet you compare me to a horse. I don't think so."

Robert knew when he was bested. "'Twill be hard riding to Highworth. We should be on our way. We will only stop to rest the horses. Can you keep up?"

She huffed. "I think you've insulted me enough for one day." And as she turned away, he thought he heard her mumble, "I'm going to hate you until my last breath."

The men jeered, teasing Elizabeth as they rode. They compared each other to their horses until finally she laughed. Told one of the men his horse was much better looking than he. No matter how Robert tried, she would not speak to him.

He decided he would let her remain angry for the day. Tomorrow. Tomorrow he would apologize. Explain he was paying her a compliment. Tell her how he found her more beautiful than all others. That none before her mattered. And tell her why he could not keep her. Why he kept pushing her away.

Tomorrow.

Chapter Twenty-Six

Elizabeth kept up the silent treatment for two days. The only time she and Sunshine had ever gotten in a fight, Elizabeth didn't speak to her for a week. Sunshine would call, and Elizabeth would answer the phone but not say a word. Funny thing; she couldn't even remember now what she was angry about. But with Robert? What wasn't she angry about? The guy had been a jerk from the moment she woke up to find him snuggling her. In all fairness, she supposed he was just as surprised to find her in the bed as she was to find him, but still...then he'd do something nice like ride to her rescue, taking out bad guys who had rape on their minds. He'd sent for a bath. And he brought her clothes, knowing she wouldn't want anything of Radford's touching her skin.

All the riding had made Elizabeth tired and cranky.

All day and part of the night they rode, only stopping to let the horses rest. Would her thighs ever stop aching? Each time she dismounted, she still felt the gentle movement of being on the back of a horse. When sailors came back from a long journey at sea, she imagined they felt the same, the rolling of the ship under their feet while they were on land.

They all slept next to the fire. One of Robert's men ended up so close to the flames, he woke to find half his hair singed off. Gavin slept curled up against her, like Elizabeth's own personal heater.

With no sign of Radford's men, Elizabeth hoped he'd decided she and Gavin weren't worth bothering about... but he didn't seem like a man who accepted losing gracefully. Maybe he was waiting until the weather broke, then he would show up all puffed up and self-important, demanding them back. Then what? Would Robert hand them over? No way she was going back. The uncertainty of the woods and the road would be a better choice. Though she still had to figure out how to help the serving girls, and wanted to talk to little Janet and see if she was speaking yet. Would she mess up history if she tried to start a women's rights movement?

On the third day, she could tell by the men's moods and the way the horses picked up the pace they must be getting close to Highworth. Time to let up on the silent treatment. Robert had tried to make her laugh. He'd even whispered in her ear in Norman French, words that sounded nice but probably were him telling her she looked like a pig and a cow. She'd pretended he wasn't there.

Gavin and Robert's knights found the whole thing hysterical. Elizabeth wasn't mad at them, so at least she had plenty of people to talk to during the trip. But whenever Robert asked a question or spoke, she acted like she didn't hear him or see him, even going as far to bump into him on her way to wash. It was immature, but it sure made her feel better. It would go under "finding the fun in any situation." Robert grumbled but took it well, which earned him a check in the plus column on her "hate him or like him" list.

Sunshine would have reminded her about the boy who pulled her pigtails when they were in first grade. Little boys thought being mean to little girls was a good way to let them know they liked them. Could Robert be the same? Was his treatment of her a mask for how he really felt?

While they rested, a few of the men talked about the wenches from the night before.

"Nothing like ending a fine meal with a fine woman." The knight with blond hair and dimples laughed.

Robert smirked. "You should be grateful I only have eyes for Elizabeth, otherwise I would have taken them all for myself."

The tall knight slapped Robert's shoulder. "The church says we should not be greedy."

"And deprive the ladies of my charming self?"

Elizabeth snorted. "Oh please. You and your big ego. I'm surprised your head can fit through the doors of the castle. Give it a rest. Everyone knows you're hot. But pretty on the outside isn't pretty on the inside. You're uglier than Radford on the inside."

The men hooted and hollered. Gavin sat on a fallen log, laughing silently, shaking so hard pieces of the log broke off and fell into the snow.

Robert placed a hand over his heart, pretending to swoon. "Oh, my lady. How you wound me."

She stuck her tongue out at him.

"Finally. She speaks. And smiles. It only took three days." Then his face grew serious as he leaned in close so the others wouldn't hear. "Truly, I am sorry. I've been an utter arse. You're beautiful and kind."

Gavin was leaning so far forward, straining to listen, that he tumbled off the log into the snow. He popped up. "I'm unharmed."

Robert's knights pretended to ready the horses, but they were completely silent, listening to what she'd say. Elizabeth knew she'd caused discord in the group, but she was tired of the way he behaved. Time to throw him a bone. She poked him in the chest and put on her *I'm here to fight the big, bad coal company* look. It usually intimidated pretty well.

"It's all fine and good to *say* you're sorry. But you have to earn forgiveness. With actions, not words. So we shall see. Perhaps in time I will believe you."

Gavin glared at Robert. "'Tis not the behavior of a chivalrous knight, my lord."

Robert ruffled the boy's hair. "You are correct, Gavin. I have not been kind to our lady. I will endeavor do better, starting this moment, in front of all these witnesses." He looked the boy up and down, then reached into his boot, pulling out a dagger.

"I'm giving you one of my daggers so you can protect your lady. Do you accept this duty, Gavin?"

His whole face lit up. "I do. Will you teach me to fight?"

The tall knight who was scary good with a sword picked up Gavin, throwing him over his shoulder. "Aye, I will teach you to take a man down with one blow."

How easily little boys could be bought. But Elizabeth didn't say anything, not wanting to ruin Gavin's happiness.

"'Tis a most wondrous gift, my lord. I will treasure it." He knelt in the snow at her feet, holding the dagger out, across the palms of his hands. "I vow to defend you with my life, lady. I swear it."

"Thank you, Gavin." She touched him on the cheek. Moments like this made her want to stay in the past. Create a life here and find out what adventures awaited. But how would she make a living? Where would she live? Gavin and some of the others she'd met were quickly becoming friends. If not for Robert and his ability to get under her skin, she'd have no doubts at all.

Then she had to turn away. There was dirt or something in her eye. Of course that's all it was.

Chapter Twenty-Seven

As they rode toward home, Robert was happier than he'd been in days. He'd finally gotten Elizabeth to speak to him. In worrying for her safety, he'd been a dolt. Never in his life had he treated a woman as poorly as he'd treated her. The choice to treat her thus to protect her was a difficult one.

If Connor was discovered, she would have no one to turn to. Her family wasn't born yet. The thought gave him pause. For weeks he'd looked for a way to protect her. He'd considered sending her to a convent. Even his gold would not save her if they called her witch. She cared so much about others that she gave herself away as odd. Ofttimes she watched his men and the people they encountered for the way to speak, to behave. She tried to fit in. Though he ached to tell her not to try.

He cared for her as she was. Wait until she met Anna and his brother Henry's bride, Charlotte. Robert wanted to see the expression on her exquisite face when she came face to face with others like her. 'Twas one thing to hear there were other future girls and another to meet them.

Thank the heavens she had changed the color of her hair. It would help her fit in. Though he would not admit it, Robert had grown used to the pretty, pale colors. With her hair darker, the freckles across her nose stood out. He ached to reach up and touch each one, connecting them to each other like stars in the heavens.

He considered sending her to Edward or one of his other brothers. But if he did, he would have to explain about Connor. And there was the other part. How did he tell John he was to blame for so much death?

He'd been brooding until she'd spoken to him today. It was like the storm clouds cleared and the sun came out. One smile from her and he wanted nothing more than to make her smile again. To see her happy.

They made one last stop to rest the horses. As he made his way back from a stream, he heard shrieking. Sword drawn, he ran...and skidded to a stop in the snow. They were not under attack. As he stood there gaping, a ball of snow hit him in the face.

Brushing the cold away, he watched as Elizabeth bent down, cupping snow in her gloves and forming a small ball. Then she threw it at Gavin. It hit the boy in the arm, and he yelped before quickly bending down to return the volley.

She hit one of his men, and soon it was a melee. Unable to resist, Robert threw a ball of snow, hitting one of his men in the shoulder. They ran to and fro, laughing, throwing snow at each other. At last, Elizabeth threw her hands up.

"I'm done. You guys win." She sat by the fire, breathing heavily. "Remind me to start spending time in the lists. Not only do I need to know how to use a sword, it seems my aim could use some work as well."

The men joined her, calling out insults to each other. Steam rose around the circle as the fire dried their clothes. What had he done with the endless days before she appeared in his life? Robert used to be content being idle all day. Hunting and drinking. But since Elizabeth had shown up, he hadn't looked at another wench. Hadn't been interested in a single one. For every time one showed him her ample assets or sat on his lap, all he could see was hair the color of the evening sky and eyes the color of the winter trees. She had turned his life upside down. Made him question his beliefs. Had ruined him for all others.

No matter how much he fought in the lists or rode, he was restless. As if some part of him were missing. Might Elizabeth be the missing part of his soul?

Did he have the right to risk her very life because he wanted her? The healer Abigail would have plenty to say about this future girl. She would say he should not have tempted the fates. That they had sent him exactly what he asked for. But he must send her back to ensure nothing happened to her. Forget her to keep her secure. The fates could hang.

It had started snowing again. Elizabeth rode close to him. "You asked me where I was from? How I ended up in your...chamber?"

He had asked her many times. Every time she'd refused to answer. Of course, she'd been angry with him or not speaking at all. He would not make her angry again, and he desperately wanted to hear the tale, have her tell him about her time. When she told her story, did he tell her he already knew from whence she came?

Elizabeth looked at Gavin to find him asleep. She spoke softly. "One of your men told me the year. 1333."

He knew what she was going to say, and yet he wanted to tell her not to speak. For saying it out loud would make everything real. And he would be honor bound to help her go back to her own time. Would have to tell her about the others. Let her go.

Her normally golden skin paled until it matched the winter landscape. She looked at him from the corner of her eye. When he didn't speak, she fidgeted in the saddle, turning her head to meet his gaze, searching his face. He had to strain to hear her words.

"I went to sleep one night in November of the year 2016. I woke in the same bed but you were beside me. It took me a while, but I accepted I'd somehow fallen through time." She looked away and looked back at him, her eyes pleading for him to believe her. "I'm not a witch or a faerie. I'm from the future."

"2016. 'Tis a very long time from now. You were in my castle? It still stands in your...future?"

She nodded. "It does. It's part of why I was so confused. Even your room looks almost exactly the same. There are small changes to the castle, so at first I didn't understand what had happened."

Robert blew out a breath, making his decision. "When we arrive at Highworth, after all are settled, we will have speech, you and I. There is much to discuss."

Chapter Twenty-Eight

Talk about anticlimactic. Robert's reaction wasn't all what Elizabeth expected. She thought he'd cross himself. Call her witch. Faerie. Throw her in a medieval insane asylum or back in his dungeon. Anything but act like he actually believed her.

If she had been given a hundred guesses, no way would she have picked acceptance. Well, he was right about one thing: they certainly did have much to discuss.

After supper she went to her chamber and found gifts waiting. A cloak so beautiful it looked like it belonged in a museum. Embroidered within an inch of its life. The wool was a deep blue, trimmed with fur, and amongst the embroidery, she touched gems used as flower centers. Who put diamonds on a cloak? There was also a new dress and shoes. Another embroidered ribbon for her hair. The optimist part of her jumped up and down. *See, if he truly wanted you to stay with Radford, why would he have gone to the effort and expense of gifts? He does like you.*

As she picked up the cloak, another ribbon fell to the floor. The room started to spin. While she knew it could be coincidence, deep in her heart she knew this was what had brought her back. It was a linen hair ribbon, embroidered with bright pink thread. In the future, the ribbon was little more than a scrap, so worn it was soft as her childhood pillowcase. She ran her fingers over it, marveling at the bright pink thread and stiffness of the fabric. Feeling silly, Elizabeth held it up to her heart, closed her eyes, and wished.

"Take me home. Where I am meant to be."

Eyes closed, she counted to twenty-one then opened them, listening. The room looked the same. Voices from the corridor made her turn. The tall knight with the deep, booming voice called out to Thomas.

Everything was the same, except she was slightly out of breath. Oh well; perhaps it was all part of the universe's plan. Living in medieval England would be the adventure of a lifetime. Elizabeth only wished she could tell her parents. They'd be so excited. A snort escaped. Of course, they'd probably try and change history. Righting wrongs as they traveled around the world.

It took a moment for the sound to register. The same noise she'd heard before. Coming from the corridor. Opening the door, she closed her eyes and listened. It was coming from the same door as before. But this time there was no guard. And no nosy Gavin. The boy was probably shadowing Robert or following Rabbie around. Leaning down, she pressed her ear to the keyhole, listening.

She'd recognize that deep burr anywhere. In all the time she'd been here, Elizabeth hadn't run into another Scot. If he was a prisoner and rated a room rather than the dungeon, Robert was going to get a cup of ale poured over his head.

The man cried out. What if he was hurt? Only one way to find out. The door opened without a sound, surprising her. Last time she'd tried, it had been locked and guarded. A man thrashed in the bed, and from the looks of him he hadn't shaved in days.

The words came again. The lines around his mouth tightened, fists clenching at the covers. It was cold in the room, but she could see a fine sheen of sweat covering his face and bare chest, and the skin was flushed. Elizabeth stuck a finger in the bowl of water. Good; it was cold. Dipping the cloth, she ran it across his forehead and face. He snarled in his sleep—Gaelic, if she had to guess.

She placed a hand on his chest. "You're safe. No one will harm you." He tensed and she brushed the black hair back from his face. "I'm here. Let go of the nightmare. I won't leave you."

At the sound of her voice, he stilled. Over and over she dipped the cloth into the water, gently running it over his face and chest, staying close, talking to him in a low voice. Telling him of her life before. How much she missed Darla and Sunshine. Words that meant nothing to him, but the tone was soft and soothing, and that was all that would matter in his fevered dreams.

Sunshine would have been drooling. He was an incredible specimen of a man. Easily over six feet tall, heavily muscled, with long hair and dark lashes. But was she attracted to him? Nope. Not one tiny bit. Elizabeth appreciated him as she would a sculpture in a gallery, but that was it. She blew a strand of hair out of her face. Was she some kind of glutton for punishment? Her traitorous heart belonged to the little boy who pulled pigtails and told her she looked like a horse or a cow. Elizabeth imagined Robert as a child. Running around, charming all he met. Brandishing a sword. She'd fallen hard. Too bad he couldn't stand her.

As she chewed on her lip, a cough made her jump. Dark blue eyes looked up at her.

"What are ye, then? Angel or devil?" He groaned. "If it's all the same, I'd rather not end up in hell. Too many enemies waiting."

She snatched her hand from his chest, heat flooding her face. He cracked an eye open, and a dimple appeared in the side of his face.

"I'm neither angel nor devil. My name is Elizabeth." She gestured to the door. "I'm sorry about coming in without knocking, but I heard you call out. The fever..."

"Connor. Pleased to meet ye, lady." He looked to the pitcher. "Might I have a drink?"

She blinked at him. "You drink the water? I thought it wasn't good."

"Nay, the water at Highworth is clear and sweet...like you, lady."

"Flatterer." She poured him a cup, licking her lips.

"The well is deep and clear." The man chuckled. "Drink your fill, lassie."

Elizabeth hadn't had water since they'd been on the road. It was cool and delicious, reminding her of the well water at Darla's horse farm back in Kentucky.

"Oh, that's good. I'm so glad you told me. I've drunk more wine since I've been here than I have in my whole life."

"You have a strange way of speaking, lass."

"I'm not a faerie or a witch. I'm from...far away."

"I dinna say you were. But you have an odd manner of speech."

"Well, so do you." His laugh gave way to a wet-sounding cough. She pressed a hand to his forehead. "You should rest."

He sat up in bed, the sheet falling to his waist, providing her with a glimpse of an impressive six-pack, deep enough she could probably run her fingers in the ridges. Did Robert have the same six-pack from all the fighting? She'd been so angry when he'd groped her that she couldn't remember, and it was dark in the chamber. Best not to think about what she couldn't have.

"I am a Scot. A mere fever will not keep me abed."

She handed him more water. "Whatever you say. If you don't mind me asking, why are you here? I thought England and Scotland were at war?"

The man turned his head to the door and settled back in bed, a smirk on his face. This couldn't be good.

Robert barged into the room. "Elizabeth. You should not be here."

"She couldn't resist my charming self." Connor touched her hand. "I think I'll keep her."

"I'm sorry. It sounded like someone needed help, so I came in. The door wasn't locked."

Robert gritted his teeth. "Remove your hand or lose it, Connor."

The man winked at her but removed his hand.

Oh, so now he was jealous. Didn't it figure? "Connor was telling me why he's here."

Robert made a noise in the back of his throat. "The dolt was injured. I took him in so he wouldn't die on my steps or bleed on the carpets."

"He owed me a debt."

"'Tis true." Robert touched her shoulder. "You must not tell anyone he is here."

"Aye. I am a wanted man," Connor said. "There is a price on my head if you're in need of gold."

"No. If I need any, I'll just steal Robert's." She touched Robert's arm. "You have my word. I won't say anything. You've been hiding him since I arrived, haven't you?"

"He arrived in the dead of night. Other than Thomas..." He looked over his shoulder. "Come in, imp."

Gavin circled the room, his eyes never leaving Connor. "He's big."

Elizabeth bit her cheek. If she laughed, Robert would pout.

"No one else knows he is here. We must keep it that way." Robert caught Gavin by his tunic. "That means no telling Rabbie or Joan or anyone else."

"I won't tell." Gavin tentatively approached the bed. Elizabeth watched as he looked Connor over, noticing the interest as the boy took in the man's muscled chest and abs. Robert caught her looking and made a face.

"You should not be undressed in the presence of a lady."

Connor arched a brow. "I find her company most pleasing. Perhaps she prefers me to you."

Robert snorted. "Do not drool on her."

"I have imposed on you overlong. I should go." Connor shifted in the bed.

Elizabeth looked to Robert and shook her head. "He can't. He has a fever."

"'Tis nothing."

Robert looked out the window. "You cannot leave. It's snowing. Likely to continue for a while."

Connor made a sound in the back of his throat. "I am tired of these four walls, pretty as they may be."

"We cannot take the risk." Robert pursed his lips. "Elizabeth or Gavin may escort you to the battlements." Then he poked Connor in the stomach. "You have grown fat and soft lazing about. No doubt you will freeze your arse off, tumble over the walls, and leave us in peace."

"This is how he shows affection," Connor told her, looking insulted. "We Scots are a hardy bunch, and if anyone has run to fat, 'tis you."

Elizabeth stood. "That's it. I'm leaving before the two of you end up brawling on the floor."

Chapter Twenty-Nine

Robert left Connor, telling Gavin to stand guard until one of the men came to relieve him. He cursed, knowing he was the one who'd left the door unlocked. He'd been distracted by Elizabeth. The Scot had looked much too interested in her. He felt something within call out, *Mine*.

Now she knew about Connor, Robert could make her understand why he had treated her thus. He went in search of her, finding her in the ladies' solar, looking like she belonged. His heart broke open. She was his. No matter the cost.

They sat on the floor sorting through thread. He stood in the doorway watching. One day perchance they would have a daughter. Janet was showing her how to embroider.

"It's no use. I'm hopeless." Elizabeth held out a piece of fabric for the girl to see. Janet pointed and shook her head.

"Easy for you to say—look at your perfect stitches. Mine look like a hedgehog ran all over the fabric."

The girl grinned. Robert watched as Elizabeth talked to Janet as if the girl spoke back to her. He crossed one booted foot over the other, arms crossed, as he listened to Elizabeth talk.

A big orange striped cat strolled into the room as if he owned the place. The cat went to Janet and curled up in the girl's lap.

"What did you name him?" Elizabeth paused. "I think he looks like a Tom. What about you?" The child nodded. A small hand tugged at Robert's arm. He put a finger to his lips.

"I'm spying."

Gavin peered into the room and turned bright red. So it was like that, was it?

"Where did Janet get a cat? I thought you said no animals in the castle?" The boy scowled. "Other than the rats."

"Shh, listen and we will find out."

"How many rats has he caught this week?"

Robert leaned forward to see Janet hold up four fingers.

Elizabeth sounded suitably impressed. "Four. Already? He's a prodigious killer, isn't he?"

The girl shook her head, her hair bouncing. The grin stretched across Robert's face. Both women had their hair in—what did Anna call it? A horse's tail? No, a ponytail.

Then the traitorous woman leaned close to the girl. "Don't tell Robert about Tom. We'll wait until he has dispatched a pile of rats. Then we show him how wonderful Tom is, and of course he'll let you keep him."

The cat purred as the girl stroked the fur.

"But you might not want to tell him we give Tom a bit of milk for bringing us the bodies." Elizabeth pursed her lips. "I know: we'll tell him it's Tom's payment."

Gavin rolled his eyes at the same time as Robert.

The two ladies giggled. "You might as well come in, instead of standing in the doorway gaping like a fish on the bank."

Gavin ran away, leaving Robert alone. The coward. So he made them both a bow. "I did not know we had a new position at Highworth."

Janet turned her face up to him.

"Head rat catcher." He pretended not to notice the cat, whom he suspected might be part dog, as large as the beast was. How much milk were they giving him?

"Would you know of anyone for the job?"

Janet pointed to the cat.

"Ah. Tom, is it?"

She bobbed her head.

"May he serve Highworth for many years." Robert

squatted down to look the cat in the eyes. One green eye opened. “I better not see loads of kittens come spring.”

The cat yawned and closed the eye. So much for Robert being the lord of Highworth.

Elizabeth had a hand over her mouth to keep from giggling.

“Perhaps I should acquire a few more cows. Tom looks like he drinks a great deal of milk.”

That did it—his lady laughed out loud. And the most wondrous thing happened. A tiny gurgle escaped from Janet’s mouth. Elizabeth’s eyes widened.

“You laughed. Can you say anything?”

The child screwed up her face in concentration, opened her mouth, and nothing came out. Her face fell.

Elizabeth leaned over to hug the child, mindful of the cat. “Don’t worry. I know you’ll be talking soon.”

Tom’s tail twitched and he bolted off the girl’s lap. They heard a squeak, and a fat, dead rat was deposited at Robert’s feet.

He reached down to stroke the beast. “How about a fish for dinner?”

The cat rubbed against his legs and stalked out of the room, the child close behind.

“Can you believe Janet laughed?” Elizabeth’s cheeks were pink, her eyes sparkled, and he thought he’d never seen such a beautiful woman in all his score and five years.

“Where did the cat come from?”

"I've no idea. He just showed up, following Janet around. We've been finding corpses ever since. I'm hoping the rats get the message and leave."

"Elizabeth?" He sat on the carpet next to her, stretching his legs out.

She'd gone still. "Yes?"

"Connor is wanted by my king. To have him at Highworth is treason. I would end up in the tower. My title, lands, and gold would be confiscated by the crown, and I would be hanged." He idly fingered the threads Janet left behind. "You would have been left alone with no one to aid you. My brothers would be in the same danger; 'tis why I have refused to see them...why I have treated you ill."

"Wait. Connor has been here since I arrived. How did you know I have no one?"

He did not want to reveal he'd known from the start she was from the future. Not yet. She would be furious, and he liked her happy.

"You did not ask for your sire and had no servants or clothes with you. I assumed."

She searched his face then nodded. "Connor is getting better. Will he just sneak out in the middle of the night?"

"There is a tunnel under the castle. He will leave and make his way back to Scotland. My debt will be fulfilled." Robert explained the debt he owed the Scot.

"I think the risk you take is worth it. But I wish you

would have trusted me enough to tell me."

"I am sorry."

"That's why you sold me to Radford? Because you thought I couldn't take care of myself? He could have raped me."

"At the time it was my best idea."

"Your idea sucked." She waved a hand. "Never mind. I'm not going to explain it."

He grinned. "I think I understand." He tucked a stray lock of hair behind her ear. "You are most beautiful."

"Like a cow?" she said, smiling sweetly.

"I will beg your pardon the rest of my days."

She held up a hand. "Like I said before, actions speak louder than words, so let's see how it goes."

With his most charming smile, Robert took her hand in his, kissing each finger. "I will woo you until you believe I care for you my breathtaking lady."

Chapter Thirty

Over the next several days, Robert took Elizabeth with him to meet those he was responsible for. He had neglected his duties far too long.

"She is good for you." Featherton sniffed.

Robert was already up, surprising his steward that morning. "Aye. I have been a fool."

Wisely, Featherton did not reply.

Following the sound of voices, Robert found Elizabeth in the kitchen packing a basket. Janet was helping her. Gavin leaned against the wall, the dagger at his hip, and Robert suppressed a grin.

"Ready?"

Gavin straightened up. "Aye." The boy cast a longing look at Janet before following them out of the hall. In a few years Robert would wager Rabbie and Gavin would be married to their lasses. Now if he could convince Elizabeth she was the one for him...

Ever since he'd found her with Connor, his fear had left him and he wondered why he'd been such a dolt. If only he'd told her before, he might have saved them all trouble. If only he'd been honest with her, told her about the other future girls. If. A small word that wielded such great power.

His people had accepted Elizabeth as their lady. He spoke quietly to them then watched her. How kind she was to every person. She truly wanted to know about their daily lives. Part of him knew 'twas because she had a need to right the wrongs of the world. A woman held up her babe for Elizabeth.

"She is beautiful. Is there anything else you need?"

The woman smiled shyly at her, casting a glance toward Robert.

"Nay, lady. Lord Highworth is good to us."

Ever since he claimed her as his wife at the inn, he'd thought about making her his forever. Connor would leave soon, and then Robert would invite his brothers to meet her. Then he would let her see for herself the others like her. The longer she stayed in his time, the longer he believed she was meant to be here by his side.

Henry's wife had told him there had been a moment she could've gone back, but she made the choice to stay. Though Charlotte did not know if it would be the same for anyone else. Her sisters said the same.

Anna had told him something different. She had been taken to see her parents, who had passed on. So he wondered if the experience was different for each person. From what his brothers had told him, he wondered why anyone would want to stay when there were such wondrous sights and things in the future.

So each day he tried to do something nice for her. Tried to make up for his behavior. Show her he cared. They'd been trapped inside by the weather for almost a sen'night. Connor paced around the castle, spending so much time on the battlements that Robert was surprised he had not turned to snow. And spending so much time above, Robert could no longer keep his presence a secret. Elizabeth told him to tell everyone at the castle. They would keep his secret if he asked.

So he had gathered everyone in the great hall for a feast. Presented Connor as a loyal friend. And said that friends were friends, no matter the country of their birth. There were a few grumbles, but in the end they'd accepted the big man. Connor kept to himself, knowing not all were happy he was at Highworth.

Robert found him most nights in the solar, reading. Elizabeth was there too, with her nose buried in a book. Gavin guarded his lady, and Janet and Tom the cat kept her company. Every time she laughed at something Connor said, Robert wanted to plant his fist in the man's face. And that was when he knew. He loved her. Had fallen the moment he woke to see emerald eyes.

“My last knightly deed was three years ago. John and his lady were imprisoned in the tower.” ’Twas unseasonably warm as Robert walked next to Elizabeth on the battlements. For once he had her to himself.

“Tell me the rest.” She pricked her finger with a needle. “Damn.” She stuffed the fabric in the pouch at her waist. “Don’t tell Janet. I’m hopeless.”

“Your secrets are safe with me, lady.” He took her finger in his mouth, tasting salt and copper as she turned a fetching shade of pink.

“John was rather infamous. We thought him dead for a long time. He had let us believe it, not wanting to bring further shame upon the family. But he had become the bandit of the wood. Preying on rich nobles and giving their gold and jewels to those who needed help. But then he was captured and thrown in the tower.”

“What happened?”

Her nose was pink as they stood looking out over the grounds. The weather had cleared, and it was the first time the sun had been out in days. She’d wanted to be outside to "take the air," as she called it.

"A woman wanted revenge on John. She was the king's mistress, then cast aside. Her husband blamed John." He caught Elizabeth's eye and held up his hands. "You think Radford was bad, he was nothing compared to Denby."

They walked back and forth, nodding to the guard on duty. "Anna spoke with the king. She was able to gain a pardon for John. Of course, she thought he was dead at the time."

"Wait. What?"

She had her arm tucked in his, and he could've walked forever with her next to him. He continued to tell her the tale. How happy his brother was with Anna.

"But then, about two years ago, I made a dreadful mistake." Robert paused, unsure of how to go on. Caring what she would think of him. Worried she would think less of him. And she should, for what he had done.

She took his hand in hers and looked up at him. "I find it's always better if you tell someone. I give you my word: I will not judge. You can tell me anything."

Robert took a deep breath. "I was on the coast. Hunting and wagering."

"Drinking and wenching." She grinned at him. "I know how this goes."

And she gave him what he needed, her acceptance, and it was enough for him to tell her the rest.

"One night I was deep in my cups. A minor noble

asked about John. Or rather the bandit of the wood. Several of the men there had been relieved of gold and horses at my brother's hands. John almost died," he said quietly. He was about to go on when he looked at her. Her lips were a very pale pink, and he knew it was time to bring her inside.

"Let's go into the solar, where the fire can warm you. I've let you remain outside far too long."

She took a deep breath. "It's so nice to be outside in the fresh air, but you're right, I'm freezing. Let's go inside."

"It's about time. I'm freezing my arse off," Gavin said as he followed behind them. Elizabeth leaned over and hugged him. Robert knew it would only be another year at most before the boy no longer wanted to be mothered. But now he leaned into her touch as if he craved it.

"Go see the cook. We're having tarts with supper. Tell him I said you could have one."

Gavin ran past them, calling out over his shoulder, "I'm telling him you said two because you made me freeze."

When they were settled in the solar, Robert saw her looking at him, waiting for him to continue the tale. He tried to stop pacing, but he was restless. Needed movement to think.

"Anna stood beside John and made a life with him. You will meet her, and I think you will enjoy talking with her." He didn't say more, wanting to finish the rest before he lost his nerve.

"Everyone was looking to me, and so I boasted. There was a woman." He pressed his lips together, looking up at Elizabeth. But her face remained the same. He saw no censure in her gaze.

She nodded to him. "Go on. I'm listening. There's always a woman, isn't there?" He was about to protest when she said, "I'm only teasing. Tell me your story."

"The night I…spent with the woman, she told me of the camp. And the keep where she and others now lived. The survivors the king's men did not kill made their way to a small keep on the coast near Scotland. A few at a time were supposed to slip out, making their way back to Blackmoor, where John had promised sanctuary."

He drained the cup. "Like a child with a new sword, I boasted to all present. Being stupid enough to ignore that some in attendance had lost their pride. Would carry a grudge. One of them took the information to court."

She took the cup from his hands, putting it on a small table. She tucked her arm in his. "Let's walk down to the cellar and count the remaining casks of wine. I want to make sure there's enough to get us through the rest of the winter."

Down in the cellar, she shuddered. "Why do you have prison cells?"

"Sometimes they are needed. It is the way of the

world. But I swear to you." He went down on one knee. "I will never, as long as we live, lock you in a cell ever again."

She took his hand and pulled him to his feet. "You better not. Because if you do, I'll slit your throat while you sleep. Come." Elizabeth pulled him deeper into the darkness. "Tell me the rest."

"'Twas six months ago when I found out the cost of my boasting. Men, women, and children were slaughtered. All had gone to the woods looking for sanctuary, which John provided. And when the camp had fallen and the king's men came, they found sanctuary again in the keep. Until I destroyed those who remained." His voice caught, and for a few moments he couldn't speak. Elizabeth did not pry; she simply waited until he was ready.

"They were hunted down. And at that hunting party six months ago, the man who had taken the information to court boasted of the outcome." Robert remembered going cold upon hearing the news.

She stopped him and met his gaze. "Guilt is a terrible thing. I heard you and Featherton arguing. Is this why you have pushed your family away?"

"Connor was one reason." He let out a sigh. "I did not want to see them. For I knew they would see the knowledge of the deeds in my eyes. How could I ever look John in the eye again after what I did? How could I tell him the people he kept safe for so long were dead because of me?”

She pulled him to her, enveloping him in a hug. Comforting and providing him with a place to land.

“You did the only thing you knew how—you pushed everyone away and lost yourself in debauchery. But you know...you have to tell John what you did. He will forgive you. I know he would understand how mistakes can take on a life of their own. You said yourself, he made a mistake that cost your family everything. He would understand better than anyone else the guilt you feel. Give him a chance.”

Elizabeth hit him on the arm. “Your behavior to me was beastly. Was this the other reason you pushed me away?”

He fidgeted. “Everyone betrays. I was not sure I could trust you not to tell others about Connor, and then later, I did not want you to know the death on my soul. If my family lost everything because of me, I could never forgive myself.”

She wrinkled up her nose. “That’s a terrible worldview. Sometimes people betray. Not all the time. Not telling your brothers about the risk isn’t fair to them. They deserve to know what could happen. You let one braggart cause so much trouble.”

“You don’t understand. How could you? Where you come from there are no more titles and lands. What would you have to lose?”

She stepped back and glared at him. “Just because

we don't have titles in America doesn't mean I don't understand. There is terrible heartbreak and pain in my country just as there is here. But at least I try to make the world a better place."

With a curse, she poked him in the chest. "What have you done to earn your fortune or your title? I'll tell you what. A big, fat nothing."

As she turned to go, he pulled her back. "Wait. Before I met you, I was in darkness. Lost under a mountain of guilt. You are right—I do not understand your time, and I have done nothing with my title or gold."

He looked into her eyes, willing her to understand him. "But I want to change. You make me yearn to be a better man."

"How can I stay angry at you now?" She hugged him tight, and Robert knew he could never let her go. Could he risk her leaving if he told her about Anna and the others?

Chapter Thirty-One

"I thought my time here would be an adventure. I should have known how different things would be. There's a different kind of danger. Especially to women." Elizabeth groaned as he took her foot, rubbing her toes.

"You did well with the dagger today." He was having a dagger made for her hand, had provided an emerald for the hilt to match her eyes. The piece would be ready before the yule.

"My body would differ." She sighed and wriggled her toes. "In my time, many women live by themselves. With no man to look out for them. Others marry. But the men do not go around carrying swords." As she looked off into the distance, a sad look crossing her face, Robert opened his mouth to tell her about Anna and the others. That was until she spoke.

"But I like it here at Highworth. The countryside and the people."

"And how about the Scots? Do you like the Scots?"

Robert pushed the leg of the chair and laughed when Connor fell over. "She does not like Scots; they mew like babes when they are ill."

"A puny Englishman would have died from my injuries. Methinks she prefers me to you."

He struck Connor in the mouth, and the Scot struck back with a fist to Robert's nose. Then they ended up rolling around the floor exchanging blows until Connor turned pale.

"Honestly, you two are worse than a couple of boys." Elizabeth rolled her eyes.

Robert stood, wiping the blood from his nose, and held out a hand to aid Connor.

"I have been ill. Do not think you bested me."

Robert's mouth twitched. "So you say. When you have recovered, old woman, we will meet in the lists."

Connor snorted, turning his attention to Elizabeth. "What did you call Highworth?" He started to laugh, and Elizabeth glared at him.

"That was before."

Robert pretended to be angry. "Before when?"

She made a face at him. "When you were a—what is it you say? Right, a dolt."

He placed a hand to his chest. "The lady wounds me.

What about my home?"

She squirmed and looked uncomfortable. Stuck her tongue out at Connor, who laughed. "It looks like a cake Bridezilla designed."

He blinked at her. "Bridezilla?"

Connor roared with laughter. "She says a Bridezilla is a lass about to be married and is awful to all around her. I told her it sounds like most of the lasses I've known, even before they're married."

Robert's mouth twitched. He pressed his lips together, but it was no use. He laughed along with Connor, and finally Elizabeth joined them.

"But does that mean you don't care for my home?"

She touched his arm. "It's very beautiful. I don't know that I would've picked something so fancy, but it suits you perfectly."

Robert smirked at Connor. "See, my lady loves Highworth. Didn't the last lass you brought home run screaming? All those cold stone walls with no tapestries."

"She was prone to the vapors. The less there is on the walls, the less there is to steal."

While Robert would never admit it to Connor, he had come to value the man's opinions. He asked interesting questions about Elizabeth's time-travel adventures. And if he hadn't been a friend, Robert would have run Connor through for how he gazed at Elizabeth. But then he'd have to cut down most of his garrison. They followed her about like lovestruck lads.

He'd talked with Connor, and the man had convinced him to let Elizabeth go if she wished to return. Then the Scot clouted him on the shoulder. "She will stay, though I still say she prefers me."

"If she goes, I will run you through."

"I look forward to it."

He'd left Robert to spend time with her, knowing their time together might be ending. Perhaps meeting Anna would convince her to stay here at Highworth with him.

The next day, they were outside. Robert was showing her the gardens, though there wasn't much to see. "In spring they are beautiful."

He'd sent Gavin and Janet to help the cook make sweets so he could talk with Elizabeth. Connor had declared himself healed, and was working up a sweat in the lists. Soon he would leave, returning home to Scotland.

"I have sent a messenger to John. Asking he and Anna to visit."

She threw her arms around him. "He will understand."

"I did it for you. You have much in common with Anna." While she might be angry, he wanted to watch her face when she met Anna and figured out they were the same.

He held her, inhaling the scent of roses from the soap

she bathed with. He leaned back, looking in her eyes. The moment seemed to stretch out in front of them. Robert leaned down, lightly touching his lips across hers. Elizabeth pressed against him as he fisted her hair in his hands, lowering her down to the stone bench. She wrapped her arms around his neck, sighing into his mouth as his tongue caressed hers. How foolish he'd been to push her away. If he had not, they might be married by now.

He captured her mouth as she made a small noise in the back of her throat, deepening the kiss. Claiming her as his. Pouring out how sorry he was for how abominably he'd treated her. Letting his kisses say what he could not. All that he wished and wanted. That he would never hurt her again.

A throat was cleared once, then again, louder. "Release her, Robert. You are not betrothed." Connor stood there, hands on his hips. Robert barely refrained from striking him.

"What are you doing here? Shouldn't you be getting beaten by my men?"

"They are no match for a Scot." Connor turned serious. "You must release her. It is not proper."

Reluctantly Robert pulled away, knowing Connor was right. Elizabeth looked dazed, her lips swollen, her gaze unfocused.

Connor offered his arm. "I will be your chaperone. You will walk with me and I will keep you safe from his unwanted attentions."

"Whatever you say." But she turned and winked, and Robert felt his heart smile. They walked for a bit longer then Connor stopped. "The lass is cold. We should see her inside, settled in front of a fire. I will sit beside her."

"And find my fist in your face."

Elizabeth held up her hands. "You can sit on my left, and you on my right, Robert."

As they entered the hall, Gavin and Rabbie danced around Connor, begging him to show them how to throw a dirk.

"All right, ye wee bastards." He looked to Robert. "I will take them down to the cellar. We can practice on the empty barrels." Then he scowled. "Behave appropriately whilst I am gone."

Once they left, Robert pulled her onto his lap in front of the fire, capturing her mouth. When they came up for air, she giggled. "I'm glad you weren't as charming when I first met you."

"Why not?"

"Because I would've spent all my time kissing you." She turned a fetching shade of pink, and Robert grinned.

"As I would have you, lady." He kissed her again. Then leaned back and looked at her, running a finger down her cheek, marveling at the softness of her skin.

"I worry I cannot keep you safe here in my time."

"No one in this world can keep another safe. Safety is

an illusion that allows us to sleep at night. I am a grown woman; I accept my choices. I'm not going to waste time trying to go back. Not if there's a place for me here." Her voice went soft. "Is there something worthwhile I can do here at Highworth?"

"Is there something you wish to do, lady? Tell me, and if it is in my power to grant, I will make it so."

She looked up at him. "I want to help the women at Radford's, and any other women who may be facing the same treatment. I don't know how, but I want them to know they can say no and mean it. And somehow I want the men to respect their word. I know it might sound impossible, but that is what I would like to do."

"I can take the three women from Radford. Best him in a wager." Robert scratched his nose. "But what you ask, Elizabeth—'tis no small thing. Servants are property. Like a cow or a horse. As much as you do not wish to hear, it is the way of the world. Will take time to make these kinds of changes, if ever."

She took his hand as he marveled at how small her hand was resting inside his palm. Then she kissed the scar over his thumb. "If I'm not going anywhere, I have the rest of my life to try to bring about change. And to me that's a worthwhile endeavor. Wouldn't you agree?"

"What was the kind of woman you told me about? The ones trying to earn women the right to vote?"

"A suffragette," she said.

"Then you shall be a suffragette for the word no."

A tear fell from her eye and he caught it on his finger. "Do you weep because you are happy?"

"Happier than I've been in a very long time."

After that, there was no talking for a while.

Chapter Thirty-Two

The next afternoon there was a commotion in the courtyard. Robert pulled Elizabeth by the arm. “Come. You’re going to meet my eldest brother Edward. He’s terribly arrogant.”

“Give me a moment to fix my hair, then I’ll be out.” She grinned at him. “I think I’ve had experience with arrogant. I’ll be fine.”

The door to the carriage opened and Robert’s face fell. John stepped out, followed by Anna and then Edward. Robert could no longer avoid his brother. John reached out to embrace him, and stopped.

“What have I done, brother?”

Edward clouted him on the arm. “Yes, what have we done for you to ignore us thus? About time a messenger arrived. We were plotting to overrun your castle and pick through the remains of your larder."

Robert thought his eldest brother looked tired from battling the Scots across the border. How would he react when he met Connor? And John. He looked happier than the last time Robert saw him.

"Who have we here? Now it makes sense why you did not want us here." He bowed before Elizabeth. "I am Edward Thornton. The finest of all my brothers. Come away with me and leave this wicked man."

She giggled when he kissed her hand. "I'm Elizabeth Jones. It's lovely to meet you. I've heard a lot about all of you."

"Don't drool on her, Edward." Robert saw the look pass between John and Anna and knew they were likely thinking the same thing. Elizabeth was a future girl.

He pulled her from Edward. "Elizabeth. Meet John and Anna." As she smiled, he added, "She came to Highworth rather unexpectedly."

John took her hands in his. "Has my brother been treating you well?" At her look, he turned to face Robert. "I think I will be seeing you out in the lists, brother."

Elizabeth held her hands up. "No. We got off to a rocky beginning, but now we're all good." Robert watched the pink spread from her chest to her neck and cheeks.

Edward frowned. "Methinks we have arrived just in time, John. Robert requires a chaperone. Henry has taken Charlotte to see her sisters. Christian went along hoping to find a bride."

Anna pushed her husband out of the way. "I'm Anna. Let's leave them alone before they start brawling in the mud."

Robert watched as the two women looked at each other. Saw the curiosity in Anna's face. She no doubt wanted to hear news of her future time. And Elizabeth—she was looking at Anna as if she couldn't quite figure something out.

"Shall we go inside where it's warm?" Edward gestured to a wagon behind them. "I have brought food and wine. I was afraid your larder would be bare and your cellars empty."

Elizabeth giggled and Robert scowled at her.

"What? He knows you pretty well."

Edward threw back his head and laughed.

At that moment, Connor appeared on horseback. As he dismounted, Robert saw Edward's eyes narrow. "What is he doing here?"

Robert moved to stand between his brother and Connor, trying to prevent blood in the snow. He spoke quietly. "I owed him a life. He showed up to collect."

The blow rocked Connor back on his feet. The Scot landed a blow to Edward's side that made him swear. The sound of blows being exchanged drew the garrison knights. Soon they were calling out encouragement and slurs.

"Come on, ye wee bastard," Connor taunted as he

landed a blow. Edward swore as blood poured from his face.

Robert cleared his throat. “Might we go inside before Elizabeth and Anna take a chill?”

His brother and Connor leaned over, gasping for breath, hands on their thighs. Satisfied they were finished for now, Robert said, “Let us go inside and have speech together. There is much to discuss.” He clapped his brother on the back. “I will ask a favor, Edward. That you take Connor back with you and across the border.”

“Bloody hell,” Edward and Connor said at the same time.

Elizabeth led Anna to the solar and called for wine while Anna chattered about their journey and how excited she was to meet her. After the wine and tarts were served and the girl left the solar, Elizabeth leaned forward, her mouth dropping open.

“You’re like me.”

Anna dropped the tart but managed to catch it before it hit the floor. “I’m not the only one.”

“I knew it. Wait. What?” Elizabeth threw up her hands. “I knew there was something about you. You have to tell me everything. And what do you mean *I'm not the only one*?"

"What do you know about Henry's wife, Charlotte?"

Elizabeth swallowed a mouthful of tart. "Just her name. No way—is she like us?"

"Yep, and she has two sisters, Lucy and Melinda. They are here too. Though Lucy came through twenty years apart from her sisters."

Reeling from the news, Elizabeth didn't know where to start. She had so many questions, and she knew then Robert had wanted her to be surprised instead of telling her himself. Instead of wasting energy being mad, she was taking her mother's advice and finding the fun.

"I can't tell you how incredible it is to meet you, knowing you traveled through time too. And then you tell me there are three others." She sat on her hands so she wouldn't leap and jump around the room in glee. "This has been one upside-down, crazy adventure. I'm dying to hear how you ended up here and what year it was when you left. Oh, and then you have to tell me all about the three sisters."

Elizabeth kept staring at Anna. She couldn't help it.

"I also came from 2016. Don't know why I ended up in the summer of 1331 and you came through in the winter of 1333."

As Anna talked, Elizabeth refilled the wine. She had a feeling they were going to need it.

"One of my friends gave me the trip. Her wedding

didn't work out, and England was supposed to be her honeymoon. So she cashed in the two tickets for one and gave me the most amazing trip. I was visiting the Tower of London when it happened…and when I came to, things were different. At first I thought John was an actor."

Elizabeth giggled. "They sure are good-looking. Are the rest of the brothers as hot? I haven't met Henry or Christian."

Anna leaned forward, her eyes sparkling. "Oh yes. They are just as handsome. It's like the angels above sprinkled an extra helping of incredibly good-looking down on all of them."

"So you went through a terrible storm when you came through?"

"I did. And there was the locket." Anna leaned back in the chair, pulling a warm woolen blanket over her lap. "My experience was a little bit different, though."

"How? There was an awful storm the night I fell through time. And there was a scrap of fabric. It looked really old, so worn the pink thread faded to almost white."

"The object and the storm was the same for both of us." Anna took another one of the fruit tarts. "What I meant was the difference was more when I could've gone back." She wiped her mouth with a napkin and looked like she was trying to decide what to tell Elizabeth.

"You see, my dad was in a facility suffering from Alzheimer's. My mom had already passed. For the longest time all I thought about was going back. Even when I knew I was falling for John, I didn't want to leave my dad alone. I was the only one paying the fees of the facility. So when I cut myself on the locket, it was different than when I came through. Instead of seeing my own time again, I was sent somewhere else. Call it heaven or whatever. All I know is my mom and my dad were there and I had a chance to talk to them. And that's when I knew my dad had died. I believe they gave me their blessing, and I'm so very grateful I had that closure, didn't have to spend the rest of my life worrying I'd let my dad down. So I came back instead of going to 2016. Came back to John."

"I'm sorry you lost your parents, but I'm really happy you found someone who completes you."

Anna took Elizabeth's hand. "What about you? Robert is very smitten with you."

Elizabeth rolled her eyes. "Oh, I don't know. We have had an incredibly rocky journey. Did I tell you what happened when I first came through?" She took a big bite of the tart, finished off the cup of wine, then sat back and told Anna the whole story. How she'd woken up in Robert's bed, which she thought was her bed. How they'd taken an instant dislike to each other.

She caught Anna up on everything, from Robert using her as the prize in a wager like he would a book or a car, all the way to him coming to rescue her. And him explaining why. Trying to make up for being such a pigheaded jerk. When she finished, she sat back, emotionally exhausted.

"We've talked about me staying, but after all I've been through, I still have a few lingering questions. Not about staying here, but about my relationship with him."

"The Thornton brothers are all stubborn," Anna said. "It takes them time to come around. But he cares for you. In fact, I think he loves you, based on how he has acted. Especially when another man showed interest, like Connor did."

Anna told her all about the Merriweather sisters and how Lucy came through first.

"I still can't believe there are five of us. I'm dying to meet them."

"They are all totally Southern and fantastic. The expressions that come out of their mouths always make me laugh. I know you'll like them. They made me feel so welcome when I met them."

Elizabeth tucked the blanket more tightly around her. "Don't you wish we'd paid more attention in history?"

Anna laughed. "You have no idea. But then I wonder if it would matter. Can you really change the past? And if we were back in our own time, would we want to know the future?"

Elizabeth shrugged. "I believe knowledge is helpful, so I think I'd like to know. Though I wouldn't want to know the date of my death or my loved ones' deaths."

She sat up, the blanket falling to the floor. "If I stay, I'll live through the black plague. I just cannot imagine."

"I can't either, but this is where knowledge is good. We can help by making sure there are cats to catch the rats. Making sure everyone washes their hands. And when we know it's spreading, we try to keep people on the estates. We can only do the best we can."

Elizabeth clapped her hands together. "It's going to be a grand adventure."

"Don't you want to go back?"

"No. Remember I told you about my parents? I haven't seen them in ages, and they have no plans to come back to the U.S. for the foreseeable future. They would think this was the best trip in the entire universe, and I have to agree. The opportunity to live in another time, it's just fantastic. I want to make the most of every day I'm here. Did I tell you what I want to do?"

The rest of the day passed as Elizabeth told Anna about Radford and the women on his estate. How she wanted to help women in general. It was growing late when Featherton stuck his head in the door. "Supper is served, ladies."

Elizabeth stood and stretched. "I don't know about you, but I'm famished."

Chapter Thirty-Three

Robert listened to his brothers talk as they caught him up on their lives and what was happening at court.

"Radford is on the outs with the king."

"Serves him right, the bloody bastard."

"Ye should have run him through when you had the chance," Connor added.

Edward had grudgingly agreed to take him across the border. The Scot stood. "I will take my leave."

When he was gone, Edward narrowed his eyes. "Out with it, whelp. Tell us why you would not allow your own family at Highworth."

Robert took a deep breath and told them everything. "I did not know he would go to court and reveal the location of the keep. The people you swore to keep safe died because of me. There is so much blood on my hands that I know you could never forgive me. So much betrayal that I could not face you, brother. I cannot ask for your forgiveness but know it is good to see you."

Edward rolled his eyes but let John speak. "Many did make it to Blackmoor. You speak of betrayal, yet my actions cost our family everything. I allowed all of you to think me dead rather than see the disappointment in your faces." He clapped Robert on the shoulder. "You could not have known what would happen." John looked to Edward. "And our brother has always been one to boast."

Edward grinned. "Aye, but perhaps he is ready to settle down?"

"Yes, Robert. Settle down and take a bride." John raised the cup to Robert. "A future girl makes a wonderful bride, though she will vex you until the end of your days."

Edward pouted. "Now three of my brothers will have future girls. What will Christian and I do? 'Tis too bad Elizabeth is an only child."

Relief swept through Robert. John had forgiven him. He cursed himself for treating Elizabeth so terribly, for not talking to John sooner, and for doubting his brother would forgive him. It seemed he had much to learn. Robert knew he wanted to spend the rest of his days learning how to be a better man with a future girl who had arrived with hair the color of the evening sky by his side. Elizabeth was the only woman for him. The woman he would love, forever and a day.

Edward clapped Robert on the shoulder. “Send her with me. We all know I could woo her better, and she would prefer me as the smartest, most handsome brother. Not to mention the richest.”

“Forget it. Thank you for coming.” Robert pulled his brother into a hug, glad he was not so serious today. “You are going to visit Christian?”

Edward looked to the sky, judging the weather. “Aye. Come along and bring your lady.”

“Nay,” Robert said. “Elizabeth and I have much to discuss—besides, she might leave me for Christian.”

Connor clapped Robert on the back. “If she wouldn’t leave you for me, she won’t have any other.”

Elizabeth and Anna had their heads close together, whispering to each other. His lady hugged Anna tight. “I’m going to miss you terribly. Be careful traveling, and I promise I’ll see you again soon.”

Anna whispered in her ear, “I have a feeling we’ll be seeing each other again soon and you’ll be my sister-in-law.”

“Oh, I don’t know about that. It seems awfully sudden.”

"You'll find out that once a Thornton decides what he wants, he single-mindedly goes after it. And Robert knows he wants you. My guess is you'll be married within the month."

"Are you talking about marriage?" John pulled his wife to him, ignoring the jeers of his brothers as he kissed her soundly. Elizabeth was gratified to see the love between the two of them.

"I was just telling Elizabeth that I think her wedding will be the next one we attend, husband."

John grinned at them. "My wife is always right, so I welcome you to the family now, Elizabeth." He kissed her on the cheek. "You are too good for Robert. The lout doesn't deserve you. We've been here for a fortnight and I haven't seen him lost in his cups any of those nights. I've even seen him out speaking with his tenants. Be good to him, Elizabeth. He has a tender heart, as much as he pretends otherwise."

"I will. Sometimes we hide behind our words. I have done the same."

"Take your hands off my lady." Robert pushed John out of the way. "Thank you again for coming." 'Twas difficult to speak; mayhap he had swallowed a bug. "For everything."

"We Thorntons may not be perfect, but we are brothers, always. And family is there for you no matter what. Don't ever stop speaking to us again, hear me?"

Robert held Elizabeth close, not wanting to let her go. "You see? My older brothers are terribly bossy. Wait until you meet Christian. He is not bossy at all."

Edward walked toward them, talking to Connor. "No wedding before we depart?"

"I would like time to ask her first."

Edward rolled his eyes. "Whatever. We welcome you to our family, Elizabeth. In the spring you can meet Henry and his wife. And, of course, her sisters. I know you will have much to speak of."

"Will you be safe at your castle? Robert said you live close to the border, and I worry about the war."

Edward rocked back on his heels. "Never fear, lady. My castle is formidable. The walls have never been breached." He embraced Robert. "If you ever ignore us again, I might actually run you through."

"I'd like to see you try."

Connor held up his hands. "As much as I enjoy a good brawl, we should go." He made a face at Edward. "I cannot believe you're making me ride inside the carriage like a mere woman."

John laughed. "We must keep you hidden. Be happy he did not ask you to dress as a woman."

Connor pointed at Elizabeth. "I will not forget, lady.

’Twas your idea for me to dress as a woman.”

A giggle escaped. “I’m just picturing you in a dress. But you have to admit, it would have been a good disguise.”

He made that particularly Scottish noise in the back of his throat and climbed into the carriage. Anna climbed in after him and then John. When he caught Robert’s look, he held out his hands. “Think you I would leave the Scot alone in a carriage with my wife?”

Robert laughed. “You hear that, Connor?”

From the carriage came the deep burr. “She is lovely. Why don’t future girls appear in Scotland?”

Anna’s words were lost as John growled and shut the door. As the carriage rolled away, Robert saw the sadness on her face.

“Missing your parents?”

She sniffed. “And my friends, but it will all work out. Think what an adventure I’ll have.”

“Come inside by the fire and let me kiss you senseless.”

“I would like nothing more.”

Robert wound the brown strands of Elizabeth's hair though his fingers. He could still see pieces that were faintly purple. "Your hair is a beautiful brown. The color of leaves in autumn. I'm glad you no longer cover it up. Every time I see you, I want to touch your hair and your beautiful skin."

Elizabeth pulled the piece of fabric from her hair, letting the ponytail fall.

He touched the ribbon. "The pink is the same color as your cheeks when you blush. Just as you are now, my love."

"I'll leave my hair down, but I'm keeping your gift with me at all times." As she went to tuck it in the pouch at her waist, she stopped, frowning.

"Is aught amiss?"

"This has to be the same one. Remember I told you I found a scrap of fabric the night I ended up in your bed?"

He nodded. And cold dread swept through him at the look on her face. Before he could stop her, she pulled the brooch he had given her off the dress. Pricked her finger and touched the ribbon. The very air in the room seemed to still. The flames in the fireplace stopped moving. And Robert held his breath, waiting.

"Guess that's that. Looks like you're stuck with me."

Robert hauled her onto his lap. "Don't ever do that again. You scared me to death."

"I had to know. I think you have to want to go back."

Robert thought of everything he knew about traveling through time. “What about the storm? There is no storm today.”

“But it is raining. I would think that would count. No matter. I know I belong here.”

“With me by your side, always.” He pressed his lips to hers, breathing into her mouth, nibbling her lips as she sighed into him. Now he had only to ask her to be his for all time.

Chapter Thirty-Four

"Would you truly give up the wonders of your time? What about your family?"

Elizabeth stroked Robert's cheek. "My parents raised me to believe in finding the fun, as they called it. To embrace change and look for the adventure in even the smallest things. They were always traveling around the country. I lived with my grandmother, and she raised me to be independent. The last I heard, my parents were on their way to India for a year. I haven't seen them in several years."

As she kissed him, his cheek felt like sandpaper against her lips. The man could shave twice a day and still have a five o'clock shadow. She traced his jaw line with small kisses before sitting back in the chair. "I know they would be happy for me."

Growling, he took hold of her hair, plundering her mouth. “I could kiss you for eternity.” He ran his hands through her hair, and she remembered him telling her she looked like his horse. Now she knew he meant it as a compliment, even though it came out ugly. He’d almost succeeded in pushing her away.

“I would have liked to meet your parents. My darling Elizabeth, you have made me the happiest man in England to say you will stay.”

A knock sounded on the door. Featherton entered as she caught her breath from the kiss. The man looked the most upset she’d ever seen him. What on earth could ruffle such an unflappable man?

“My lord, lady. Best come into the courtyard.”

As they followed him down the stairs, Elizabeth heard the commotion. The voice made her stop. Robert almost ran into her back.

“It’s him.”

“One of the wheels broke on the carriage. I require shelter.” Lord Radford stood before him.

Robert landed a blow to Radford’s gut.

The man doubled over, gasping for air. “Why did you do that?” Radford hunched over, breathing through his mouth.

“That is for your treatment of my lady.”

Radford ruffled up his feathers. “Your lady? She is mine. I won her fair and square.”

“She is mine now. Consider her payment for me allowing you to stay here and provide you with a new wheel for your carriage.”

Radford huffed and puffed but agreed. Robert laid a hand on his arm. “My servants are off limits to you. I have heard you do not understand what no means.”

The man sneered at him. “The strange lass has bewitched you. Servants are ours to do with as we please.”

Robert raked a look over him. “Nay. Not at Highworth.”

A calculated look appeared in Radford’s eyes. “Shall we have one last wager, then?”

Elizabeth laid a hand on his arm. “Robert. Do not do this.”

He bent down to her, his lips close to her ear, and whispered, “Do not doubt me. I lost on purpose before to send you with him. Only because I thought I could not keep you safe. This time I will not lose, and he will never plague us again.”

He thought she would be pleased, but the fury on her face made him take a step back.

"Haven't you learned anything? When something is really important, you should not handle it so carelessly. The risk is too great—or don't you care?"

Radford snorted. "You allow a woman to speak to you thus?"

Robert shrugged away from her. "What are the stakes?"

"For her. Swords at dawn."

"Robert, don't."

He made a pretense of thinking on the offer. "She is too valuable. 'Tis not enough. I also want the three serving women. They would make a fine addition to my household. And, of course, the entire contents of your cellar. I heard you have recently acquired a large shipment of spirits."

Radford narrowed his eyes. "You have grown lazy with a blade. Too much time drinking, not enough time fighting. I accept your stakes. And if I win—which I will, make no mistake—I will take her, your horses, and your gold."

Robert inclined his head. "You are welcome at my table to eat. At dawn I will best you."

Featherton glared at him as he passed by. "If you'll follow me, Lord Radford, I'll take you to your chamber."

Robert trailed his lady to her chamber. The sooner he married her, the sooner he could wake with her every morn. As he entered the chamber, he had a moment to duck before the basin hit the wall close to his head and shattered.

"Are you insane? He could have killed me last time, and now you bet me again? Haven't you learned anything?"

"Listen to me, Elizabeth. This way I will get the women back for you. Isn't that what you wanted, to save them?"

She threw up her hands. "Not like this. What if you lose? Did you think of that? Then I will have to go with him again."

He shook his head. "I will not lose."

Robert knew he would remember her anger for years to come. The violence burnt so brightly within her that he was surprised she did not burst into flame. Why could she not see that this was the best way to free the women she wished to help? Yet she bellowed at him.

She put her hands on her hips. "But if you do? Are you not honor bound as a knight and lord to send me with him?"

Robert had to admit, she had him there. And his brief hesitation cost him.

"I knew it. You would send me back. After all we have been through. All the progress we have made. And now you act like a jerk again. I was stupid to stay here. I want to leave."

"Where will you go?" She could not leave. Highworth was her home now.

She paced around the room. "I don't know.

Anywhere but here. I'm sure someone would take me to clean for them. I'm sure I can be of use. As long as it isn't here. I don't want to live with someone who thinks so little of me he would offer me up like a piece of property."

"Elizabeth. Calm down. You will feel better after we eat." And that was the entirely wrong thing to say. She screamed and yelled at him, throwing everything she could reach. Robert decided it was best to leave. He backed out of the room, shutting the door, hearing the pitcher shatter as it hit the wood.

In the hall as Robert made his way to the table, Thomas chuckled. "I'd say that didn't go as you thought."

Robert rolled his eyes. "She does not understand. I am the best swordsman around. How can she doubt I will best him?"

Thomas blew out a breath. "For someone who knows so much about women, sometimes you know nothing. You have hurt her feelings. It does not matter if you are the best swordsman in all the land. She feels you do not value her, that you would betray her. And that is why she is so angry."

Robert hadn't even thought of it. He believed she would understand why he did what he did. "But I will get back the women she wanted to help."

"But the way you went about it is not acceptable to her. She is not like women of this time, Robert. You have made a grave mistake."

Robert let out a sigh. "She refused to come down for supper. I will wait until the morrow. If I go back in there now, she may stab me with the dagger I gave her. When I win, all will be well."

Thomas looked unconvinced. "If you say so."

Chapter Thirty-Five

Elizabeth was rethinking her decision to skip supper because she was mad at Robert. While rationally she accepted the idea, the other part of her, the part he'd hurt, rebelled. The man was making the same mistake all over again. She knew he was angry that she thought he could lose, that somehow she didn't believe in him. But it was always a possibility. Otherwise it wouldn't be a wager.

She felt like a spoiled brat when one of the servants cleaned up the mess she'd made. Elizabeth had offered to help, but they shooed her away. A replacement pitcher and basin were brought to the room, making her feel even worse for being wasteful when things were much harder to come by in this time. It wasn't like at home where you could just toss the object in the trash and go buy another. She had behaved badly, but Robert pushed her too far.

She decided things would look better in the morning, and went to bed early. A noise woke her. Where was Gavin? He usually slept on a small bed in the corner. The door to her chamber was open. In her anger, she must've forgotten to lock it before she went to bed. When she got up to close the door, there he stood.

"What have you done with Gavin?"

As Elizabeth asked the question, she saw the boy sprawled on the floor in the corridor, a candlestick on the ground beside him.

"He will live." And, quiet as a rat, Radford stepped out of the shadows, shoving her against the wall, his leg going between hers. He held her wrists so she couldn't strike him.

He leaned down, smelling like a brewery. "I will have you this night. And then I will kill that Thornton bastard for interfering."

She managed to hit his forehead with her own, making him release her. There was nowhere to go but in her room. Elizabeth backed in, searching for a weapon. Feeling like the mouse a cat took its time to stalk and play with before killing, she searched for the dagger. And she made a promise to herself. If she got out of this okay, she would keep that dagger on her at all times, even when she slept.

Radford cornered her, punching her in the stomach

so hard she doubled over, falling to the floor, gasping for air. He grabbed hold of her hair and pulled her head back, forcing her to look at him. “I will have you tonight.”

Thunder cracked, sounding like it was right outside the window. Rain made wet droplets on the window seat and floor. Lightning lit up the room and she spied the dagger under a blanket on the window seat. She reached for it, but Radford knocked it from her hand. He backhanded her and lunged for the blade.

She’d managed to get to her feet when there was pressure, then cold on her arm. Dumbly, Elizabeth looked down at the blade sticking out of her bicep. At first she didn’t feel anything, then red spread across her sleeve and pain radiated in all directions, sending her back to her knees. Gasping through the pain, she saw Janet slide out from under the bed and run out of the room.

Robert was talking with Thomas when Janet tugged on his arm.

“What is it, little one?”

She screwed up her face in concentration, but nothing happened.

"'Tis all right. Speech will come when 'tis time."

The child stamped her foot and tried again. This time a tiny sound came from her mouth. The high-pitched voice sent ice through his body.

"My lord, come now. He is killing her."

The child turned and ran up the stairs, Robert and Thomas on her heels.

He reached Elizabeth's chamber to see Gavin sprawled on the floor.

Janet took a deep breath. "I will tend him. Go."

As Robert entered the chamber, he saw Radford pull a dagger from his lady's arm and raise it above his head. Robert unsheathed his sword and cut Radford down with one blow. As the man lay there, eyes open and unseeing, he crawled over to Elizabeth. She was pale as the moon.

"My love, did he stab you anywhere else?"

Her eyes were unfocused as he helped her to sit up. "Elizabeth, where are you hurt?"

Blood seeped from her arm. Robert pulled the ribbon from her hair and bound her arm. As he did, thunder crashed, the wind blew rain into the chamber, and lightning flashed.

Before his eyes, she faded. 'Twas the only way to describe it. One moment he was holding her in his arms, the next he could still see her but no longer feel her. She was going back to her own time. In his foolishness, he had lost her.

"Nay. Do not leave me." He looked to the heavens, beseeching the fates. "I love her. Do not take her from me."

Elizabeth woke in bed.

"You were asleep for three days. I thought I'd lost you." Robert touched her hair and face as if he couldn't believe she was still there. "You lost a great deal of blood. Adeline and Janet saved you."

She tried to speak, but her throat was dry. Instead she pointed to the pitcher.

"Here, love." Robert handed her a cup of water.

"Now I know why I felt so creeped out in that chamber in my time. I almost died there."

He had sent everyone away. Told them when she woke he would let them know, but he could not leave her side to tell everyone the glad tidings. Not yet.

"I was an arse. Again." He kept touching her, unable to believe she was still here. "What happened when you faded? Did you go back?"

Elizabeth closed her eyes for a few moments. When she opened them, they were full of tears. “I saw you. You were with me.”

Fear flowed through him again. “I would not let you go. Even when I could no longer feel you, I held on.” He thought about what had happened. “I saw fantastical things. Brightly colored carriages with wheels but no horses, and people were riding in them. There was an enormous metal bird in the sky. And the sounds. So much noise I thought my head would split in two.”

He wiped his own eyes, clearing the dust from them.

She grasped his hand in hers. “When everything happened, somehow I knew why you wagered with Radford. I know you did not mean to hurt me, but to save the girls, like I asked.”

She took another sip of water. “I remember pulling against the waves of time. There were so many choices, and all I had to do was choose a time and place, but I knew deep in my heart I belonged with you. I could feel you holding my hand. Hear you whispering in my ear to come home to you. So I chose the life I wanted and I fell back to float on the current of time towards your voice. Towards home.”

Robert left not a bit of skin un-kissed. He marveled at the softness of her lips and skin.

“Forgive me and I'll never do anything so foolish again.”

“You will, but I forgive you anyway.”

He lowered his mouth to hers, and she closed her eyes and surrendered to him. Robert nibbled her lips, tasting her mouth and skin. A spark of what he imagined lightning felt like coursed between them, and a rainbow of color filled the room, reminding him of her hair before she had hidden the colors. Robert growled deep in his throat as he caressed her with his mouth, wordlessly telling her over and over how much he loved her.

When he broke the kiss, he whispered, “Actions, not words—isn’t that what you said, lady?” Robert met her gaze. “But I shall say the words anyway so you cannot pretend not to know. I love you, Elizabeth. With all my heart and soul.”

“I love you, too.” She put her arms around his neck and held on. “Forever my knight. Forever.”

Books by Cynthia Luhrs

Listed in the correct reading order

THRILLERS
There Was A Little Girl
When She Was Good

TIME TRAVEL SERIES
A Knight to Remember
Knight Moves
Lonely is the Knight
Merriweather Sisters Medieval Time Travel Romance Boxed Set Books 1-3
Darkest Knight
Forever Knight
First Knight
Thornton Brothers Medieval Time Travel Romance Boxed Set Books 1-3
Last Knight
The Merriweather Sisters and Thornton Brothers Medieval Time Travel Romance Boxed Set Series Books 1-7

COMING 2017 - 2018
Beyond Time
Falling Through Time
Lost in Time
My One and Only Knight
A Moonlit Knight
A Knight in Tarnished Armor

THE SHADOW WALKER GHOST SERIES
Lost in Shadow
Desired by Shadow
Iced in Shadow
Reborn in Shadow
Born in Shadow
Embraced by Shadow
The Shadow Walkers Books 1-3
The Shadow Walkers Books 4-6
Entire Shadow Walkers Boxed Set Books 1-6

A JIG THE PIG ADVENTURE
(Children's Picture Books)
Beware the Woods
I am NOT a Chicken!

August 2016 – December 2017 My Favorite Things Journal & Coloring Book for Book Lovers

Want More?

Thank you for reading my book. Reviews help other readers find books. I welcome all reviews, whether positive or negative and love to hear from my readers. To find out when there's a new book release, please visit my website http://cluhrs.com/ and sign up for my newsletter. Please like my page on Facebook. http://www.facebook.com/cynthialuhrsauthor
Without you dear readers, none of this would be possible.

P.S. Prefer another form of social media? You'll find links to all my social media sites on my website.

Thank you!

About the Author

Cynthia Luhrs writes time travel because she hasn't found a way (yet) to transport herself to medieval England where she's certain a knight in slightly tarnished armor is waiting for her arrival. She traveled a great deal and now resides in the colonies with three tiger cats who like to disrupt her writing by sitting on the keyboard. She is overly fond of shoes, sloths, and tea.

Also by Cynthia: There Was a Little Girl and the Shadow Walker Ghost Series.

Made in the USA
Middletown, DE
15 March 2022